A WEEK IN VIETNAM

WELCOME
TAN-SON-NHUT
USAF - VNAF
PASSENGER SERVICE

A WEEK IN VIETNAM

A Novel by William Michael Murray

Copyright © 2019 William Michael Murray

All rights reserved.

ISBN-13: 978-0-578-57124-9

This book is dedicated to
the officers of the U.S. Navy Supply Corps.
The most professional organization
I have ever been associated with.

If you go into a madhouse and intend to return ...
take love with you.

TABLE OF CONTENTS

FOREWORD

WILLIAM MICHAEL MURRAY'S, *A WEEK IN VIETNAM,* draws me back to 1972 into that strange neverland of time just shortly before our troops were called home. American families were down to their last raw nerves, and even those were being jumped up and down on by years of controversial military involvement. My childhood friends' fathers were away at least a year at a time, while their mothers remained behind. Families put check marks on calendars each day their loved ones were away, all bringing them one step closer to an anxiously awaited homecoming. Time moved like turtles in mud, each moment a pendulum that chimed on a clock of angst over a loved one's whereabouts and the condition in which he or she might return. Yet, some had no one at all who awaited back home. There were thousands of families that shattered into fragments like dried pecans under the hammer of wartime stress. These were made up of fathers who either couldn't or wouldn't return home, and mothers who sometimes pushed them away like strangers. American casualties were not only on the battlefields.

In Vietnam, the whirring of Huey helicopter blades replaced the gentle buzz of box fans used during sweltering summer months in Georgia. Grenades, dropped into water to scare Viet Cong, replaced the gentle sounds of three-year-old boys playing with tugboats in soapy baths in Ohio. Pale, grey, tasteless meals left men and women turning food over this way and that, looking for a better side, and were a poor stand-in for home-cooked meals of fried chicken, mashed potatoes and sweet peas in Texas. Those simple pleasures that may have been taken for granted back home in any state, became the gold standard for what really mattered.

Murray's first-person narrative gives us a bird's eye view of the life of Lieutenant Powell as he emerges from relatively bucolic island life on Guam into the uncertainty of wartime Vietnam. There pregnant prostitutes work the bars while sergeants broker black-market merchandise for personal profit. Mosquitoes and sand are as ubiquitous as the lack of sanitary conditions in some instances. Glorious memories of loves won and ghosts of loves lost hang like portraits over men's beds as they seek comfort, or at least diversion. In the midst of chaos and fear during uncertain times, many servicemen lost their internal compasses and the hope of a better day.

So, how can one supply officer survive intact?

Ultimately, it is love and a good sense of humor that pushes Lt. Powell forward and gives him faith that his own life is still worth living.

—Marci Henna, author of
When We Last Spoke, and *What Lies Ahead.*

ACKNOWLEDGEMENTS

I MUST BEGIN BY EXPRESSING my most sincere and deeply felt gratitude to my "muses", Dana Anderson and Marci Henna. Without their continuing advice, help and support I can truly and humbly admit that you would not be reading this book. It would probably have ended up in storage in one of the file boxes where my previous novel ended up.

I would also like to thank Susan Krupp of SusanArt (99Designs) for her design work on the book cover and the Title Page and the Frontispiece. Her creativity and her willingness to put up with my myriad changes made her a joy to work with.

I also need to thank Abbie Bennett for her thorough and professional edit of the book. I still smile when I think of her favorite character in the book ... the squirrel.

I also need to acknowledge the contribution of my good friend, Debra Krakar, who is the Executive Director of the Dog Alliance, who volunteered to help set up my Webpage and Facebook page. It was a true labor of love.

Last and not least, let me thank my wife, Helen Parish, for putting up with me during this odyssey.

DAY ONE

THE EXPLOSION JARRED ME AWAKE and rattled the glass of the room. We were under attack.

I sat up on the side of the bed grabbed my clothes and scanned the room to locate the rifle, an M-16, I had seen propped up in the corner. I looked over at Jim lying on the bed against the other wall for some idea of what I was supposed to do. Jim sat up dazed, looked around, then rolled over and started to go back to sleep.

One part of me didn't want to appear to be as inexperienced as I was, especially since Jim didn't even seem concerned. The other part of my brain was screaming, "We're under attack. Didn't he hear that explosion? Grab a weapon and be prepared to return fire."

Probably all lines from some Grade B war movie. Fortunately, interspersed with the movie dialogue, I did have some rational moments. Jim had to have heard it. Did he think he'd dreamed it? I sat there for a while, which seemed like a couple of hours, but was probably less than a minute.

"Jim, do we need to react to that explosion?" I finally asked. An incredibly stupid question in retrospect, but probably less stupid than the other questions I rejected.

"No," he yawned, not bothering to open his eyes to look at me. "If the Viet Cong are going to attack, we generally know because the maids don't show up."

1

That was it. That was the intelligence? The maids had come today so this wasn't an attack. I sat there for a long time coming up with possible alternative explanations, all of which began with, "Well, today was the exception. Loud explosions are generally indicative of an attack."

Since I didn't hear any other shots or anyone running and yelling, I decided that, even though there had been a loud explosion, it wasn't an attack. I finally did go back to sleep. Not easily. Not soundly. But I did sleep.

I hadn't been in Vietnam a full day yet.

It was early March 1972. I had flown into Tan Son Nuht Airport in Saigon that morning. As far as I could tell, everyone on the plane was returning to duty in Vietnam from R&R in Hawaii or some other vacation spot - except me. I was stationed on Guam and had caught this flight when it had landed there to refuel. I looked around just before we landed. The plane had gotten quiet and most of the passengers were finishing their umpteenth drink before they had to hand their empty cups to the stewardess coming around with the large trash bag. The looks on their faces were simply the looks of people resigning themselves to having to return to an unpleasant job. No joking around, no looks of fear, just resignation.

Besides wondering what I was doing on that flight and what I was expecting to accomplish when I got to Vietnam, my concern was whether I was going to actually get into the country or spend the next several days in the airport before being put on a return flight and sent back to Guam.

During the flight the soldier sitting next to me had cautioned, "This war is really fucked up."

I wasn't even in it yet, but I was already getting acquainted with the truth of that adage.

I was a Navy Supply Corp officer. Supply Corp officers run the business side of the Navy. We handle logistics and accounting.

Although we are not classified as non-combatants, and we do get a modicum of combat training, our jobs are such that we don't go "in harm's way" very often. On our collars we wear an insignia that designates us as being in the Supply Corps. Other than that, we pretty much look like regular Naval officers.

For the last two years, the length of my assigned tour, I had been working at a shipyard on Guam in a pretty cushy job. After talking to my boss, I agreed to extend my stay in the job for another year. The request was quickly approved, probably due to the fact that Guam was only slightly higher than Vietnam on the list of choice duty locations. After all, in Vietnam you could get killed from something other than alcohol poisoning or terminal boredom, which were probably the principal causes of death on Guam. I had taken a month's leave at home and had been back in the job for a couple of days when my boss told me that I was getting orders to another command on Guam. I was being assigned to be the Staff Supply Officer for a squadron of Patrol Gunboats that were still actively engaged in Vietnam. The job would require that I remain on Guam for at least another year, and probably longer. So much for my cushy job.

I stayed up late that night in order to call Washington to find out what had gone wrong. I got my detailer, the guy that issued my orders, on the phone and I started the conversation with, "What the fuck?"

His initial response was, "Well, you wanted to stay on Guam, didn't you?"

In what can best be described as constricted throat language, I told him that I had extended to stay in the job. The following conversation ensued.

"Well the officer you are relieving is a reservist and his obligation is up in a couple of months. He has to be out of the Navy by the end of February. We don't have time to find another replacement and you have the necessary qualifications for the job."

"By necessary qualifications, since I have no background or training in what they do over there, you mean that I'm the correct rank and I can feed myself, right?"

"Well, I guess you're joking, but all in all, that's pretty much right. Needs of the Navy."

"Just one more question and I'm afraid I already know the answer. I extended for a year. Is that going to be honored?"

"Nope. This is a new assignment."

The term "livid" does not adequately describe my feelings at that moment. I terminated the conversation to avoid a possible court martial. To make matters worse, on several occasions in my first job at the shipyard, I had to deny requests from the very organization to which I was now being sent. I wasn't expecting a welcome.

Strike one.

During the ensuing two months before I had to report, my wife told me that she had had enough of me and the island and that she wasn't going to stick around for another year or two. She was going home and would file for divorce.

Strike two.

The ships of the squadron that I was ordered to were Patrol Gunboats – PGs in Navy parlance. They were designed to fight in Vietnam. They were only 165 feet long and were shallow draft. The hulls were aluminum and everything above the main deck was made of fiberglass, so that bullets and rockets could pass through the ship without doing significant damage – to the ship – not necessarily to the sailors standing inside of the ship.

The ships patrolled using diesel engines, but they also had a jet engine, the same J79 engine that was used on Phantom jets. The jet engine didn't really move the ship. The exhaust from the engine was blown through a turbine which was geared to the ship's propeller. This allowed the PGs to go from zero to over 40 knots in a little over one length of the ship. The acceleration was such that the crew on the bridge sat in chairs equipped with seat belts. The ship's complement was four officers and 20 enlisted. Most of the officers were so junior that they were serving their first assignment. The ships spent their time in Vietnam patrolling the coast and going up the rivers.

The situation in Vietnam at this time could best be described as confusing. The war was being "Vietnamized," meaning more of the actual fighting was supposed to be handled by the Army of the Republic of Vietnam, the ARVN. The U.S. military was shutting down and pulling out as quickly as it could. The Navy had a large base at Cam Ranh Bay, which it had just turned over to the Vietnamese. The PGs I was scheduled to be working with were the only commissioned Navy Ships still actively engaged inside of Vietnam. There were still "swift boats" working the rivers, but they weren't commissioned ships. Since the ships needed a logistics base, they had been moved to a location on the Mekong River. All of their basic supplies, food, oil and ammunition were supposed to be supplied by the Army that had a post at that location, but that post was also engaged in shutting down. Messages from the ships indicated that they were having problems getting supplied.

The Vietnamese had begun their last major offensive operation before the war ended. It came to be known as the "Eastertide Offensive," since it was started around Easter of 1972. The entire country was now classified as an active war zone.

The situation I was going into wasn't good. I wondered if this was going to be strike three.

Despite the fact that I didn't "do" John Wayne, I knew that I was the only person that could probably help with the logistics problem and that I really should go and see if I could, at least, alleviate the situation, knowing that I probably wasn't going to solve it. So, I volunteered to go. I reiterate: I volunteered to go.

That decision began a series of communications with the Supply Officers at the headquarters of the Chief, Naval Advisory Group located in Saigon. I would be administratively assigned to them while I was there. They would assist with finding me a place to stay and getting me transportation down to the base where the ships were located. It was during this communication that I encountered the first hurdle. I received a message telling me to make sure that all of my paperwork was in order. Since I wasn't officially assigned to Vietnam, I wouldn't be coming in through the U.S. side of the bureaucracy but would have to clear Vietnamese immigration and customs. I was advised that giving Americans trouble at the airport was a favorite pastime of the Vietnamese and, for example, if my rank and my orders didn't agree, I could be held at the airport until the problem might be resolved, which could take several days. I had just been promoted, so my rank on my ID card was still my lower rank and the rank on my orders reflected my new rank. So, a few days before I was supposed to leave, I went to get a new ID card asking that it be expedited. I was scheduled to catch the flight on a Sunday morning. On Saturday I still didn't have the new ID card, and no one knew anything about it.

So, as I buckled my seat belt for landing in Saigon, I was still not sure what I was going to be doing and more to the point, whether or not I was going to spend the next several days at the airport not accomplishing anything.

I have often thought about why I volunteered to go to Vietnam. I am not the type to volunteer to undertake jobs where I can't foresee a clear path to success. I considered the possibility that I may have succumbed to what attracts young men to volunteer to go to war – glory, honor, becoming attractive to women. I was pretty sure that wasn't the case for me. By this time, I knew that this war was a mistake, and I wasn't overly enthusiastic about dying because of someone else's mistake.

I did have a sense of obligation, though. This was my job and I knew I should be doing it. On the other hand, this wasn't a job I had volunteered for, or even wanted, and I could quietly do it on Guam without the added risk that I had agreed to undertake. Boredom probably played a part. This new assignment was far less than challenging, and at that time there were over 6,000 unattached men on Guam and about 25 single women, mostly teachers, nurses and a few military. I really didn't have a social life, unless imbibing copious amounts of gin counted as a social life. At least this promised something different. Whatever the reason, I was about to land in South Vietnam not knowing if I would remain there and not knowing what I would be doing when I got there.

The plane landed at the airport in Saigon. The airport personified "chaos". I fell in line with all the military personnel who were returning. I followed them through a separate area which seemed to be designated for returning military. Since I was in uniform, no one asked for my papers. I seemed to be through.

Hurdle number one avoided.

I had the telephone number of the command I was reporting to. I located a telephone and called them. They seemed surprised that I was already through the Vietnamese bureaucracy. I briefly explained what I had done. They seemed amused and said that they would send someone over to get me and told me where to stand. In a few minutes, another Supply Officer drove up in a jeep and introduced himself as Jim.

We drove to the Chief, Naval Advisory Group Headquarters. The headquarters building was a large, rather new looking office building that abutted the Mekong River. I noticed that a destroyer that the U.S. had given to the Vietnamese Navy was tied up to a pier near the building. I recognized the ship because we had worked on it at the shipyard on Guam. Once inside the headquarters building, I followed the officer into a large, open room with several desks in it. I'm not sure what I expected, but this wasn't it. It could have been any administrative office in any location in the U.S. I was introduced to all the officers working there and assigned a desk to use while I was there. Not only was the building and room nondescript, but the officers were dressed in khaki uniforms – no camouflage, no weapons.

It was lunchtime, so I was invited to go with them to have lunch. We walked over to the senior officers' quarters nearby. We went up to the roof where the dining room was located. The quarters were at one time a hotel, probably French, and the dining room was an old, rooftop area that probably once served as a rooftop lounge. It was a good reminder that the French were there until they too learned that fighting a war in Indochina was a no-win situation.

We all sat around a large table and had the lunch meal. The meal consisted of two frankfurters, cooked so long that they were dark brown and wrinkled, along with two scoops of some undeterminable concoctions which fell under the general category of food – both of which were white. I finally decided one of the scoops was possibly scalloped potatoes, the other remains a mystery. All of this was served with a side of white bread. Three white things with two links of dark-brown, wrinkled thing. All we could do was laugh. This was the senior officers' mess and was run by the Army. I wondered what the average soldier was being fed.

One of the things that Supply Officers do is manage food service operations – most particularly the crew messes on board ships. The comment was made that if we served a meal like this aboard ship the crew would probably throw us overboard and the captain would swear we jumped.

I spent the rest of the afternoon checking in and trying to plan what I would do for the next week.

My orders were for me to be in Vietnam for a week. The orders were written for a week for two reasons. First, for me to have enough time to see if I could get something done and, secondly, because there were certain perks that came with being there for a week.

I would bunk with Jim while I was there, which eliminated the problems associated with my signing for a room and transporting me back and forth to the headquarters building.

None of the PGs I had come to assist were in port. One would be coming in in two days, so it was also decided that I would travel to the port the next day to be available when the ship did come in.

I spent most of the afternoon getting to know the officers assigned there and discussing how I might accomplish what I was supposed to do. It only occurred to me in retrospect, but the surprising thing was that these officers actually believed the reason I gave for being over there. Possibly the idea that I had volunteered to go to a combat zone, while actual combat operations were underway, when I really didn't need to, for the purpose of seeing if I could improve the logistic support for the ships that I was working with, did stretch credibility a little. I found out later that it probably stretched it a lot. However, these were all Supply Officers. We prided ourselves on being professionals. If the job required our going somewhere, we'd go.

I soon found out that all the officers had volunteered for this duty. Nixon was trying to eliminate the draft and was looking for the military services to send volunteers to Vietnam to the maximum extent possible. Admiral Zumwalt, who was head of the Navy at the time, had sent out correspondence requesting volunteers and had offered a long list of perks to anyone volunteering. Most of them were probably intending to make the Navy a career and getting your "ticket punched" with duty in a war zone was certainly obligatory, but there was something more than that. As an officer named Bob put it, "Zumi needed officers to go to Vietnam — that was enough for me."

I'll never forget Bob. He was a tall, trim, athletic guy with a good sense of humor. He actually seemed like he enjoyed what he was doing. George, the senior officer of the group, reminded me of a partner in a CPA firm. He was quiet, pleasant and supportive, but he was going to get the job done. I found out that Jim was married, but that was about all I knew about any of them.

At the close of business Jim checked out one of the jeeps, and he and I headed for the BOQ, which stands for Bachelor Officers' Quarters. Being a bachelor is not a prerequisite to staying there. Unaccompanied quarters would probably have been a better term. The BOQ was in located in the Cholon district of Saigon and had once been a hotel. Cholon is the Chinese area of Saigon. The room was comfortable but showed its age. The shower was inside of the room and was one of those where the showerhead was attached to a pipe that came up out of the floor. The shower curtain was made to pull around you when you showered. There was a separate toilet and two beds.

Jim asked if I liked Chinese food. I did. We changed into civilian clothes and headed for a Chinese restaurant nearby. The food was good and reasonable and was a great improvement over lunch.

From there we headed to one of the now infamous Saigon bars. On the way, Jim explained the procedures. I'm not sure whether the procedure applied to all of the bars in Saigon, but it was the way that this establishment worked. The girls were available for hire, but there were no "meeting rooms" available on premises. If you fell in love and wanted companionship for the evening, you began by negotiating a reasonable fee with the girl of your immediate dreams, or maybe fantasy was the better term. When I say negotiate, the fee varied based upon the amount of time you wanted her services and what "extras" you wanted included. The negotiation always began with a price for the longest amount of time.

"For that money I love you long time."

Those words often came back to me in the midst of working out a settlement agreement during my most recent divorce. I often think that the phrase should appear in most prenups. But I digress.

Coming to an agreement on the fee was only half the financial arrangements that were necessary. You also had to "buy her out of the bar." The bar made money on you buying drinks for the girls. If you were going to take the girl out of the bar, then you had to compensate the bar for the lost revenue. For this you negotiated with the mama-san. At this point you were at a distinct disadvantage because you were now negotiating with the mama-san who was explaining how much money they would lose by your taking one of their "best girls" out of the bar. If what qualified one as a "best girl" could be defined, I think it was measured by the amount of money that a girl could generate by having you buy her lots of expensive drinks. On the other hand, maybe it was a generic term that covered all of the girls. I should also note that even though I saw many girls downing lots of expensive drinks, I never saw one drunk.

As you haggled over her value, your now intended kept reminding you of the hours of erotic pleasure you were missing because you were taking too much time with the mama-san.

"You a rich GI. Just pay her. You missing number-one pussy!"

Assuming that you had successfully run the financial gauntlet, there was still the problem of the room. Taking your intended to the BOQ was probably out of the question. I never actually asked that question, because the distance involved made it a non-starter. Happily, your intended always knew of a place. Some more money.

So, I now knew the rules. However, Jim and I had agreed that we needed to be at work early, so we would only stay for a couple of beers. No "long time" tonight.

We entered the bar. The place could best be described as Asian-Disco Fusion. Bright colored lights, disco balls, Chinese lanterns and blaring disco music. If this décor was intended to stimulate my erotic-bone – sort of like a funny-bone, but with a different physical reaction – it failed miserably. However, since I was in my twenties, my erotic-bone really didn't need much external stimulation in the way of bright, colored lights and loud music. We walked over to the bar and ordered a couple of beers. Two girls walked over and struck up a conversation.

The girl that approached me was small, petite and cute – I think. She looked about 16 but was no doubt older. The thing about her that first caught my attention – and held it – was that she was at least seven months pregnant. Seriously. She was wearing hot pants, the waist band of which was under the bump and for a top she wore what could best be described as a baby-doll top, which covered her boobs but parted at her stomach. Almost like a curtain on a stage – parted at the center to show the set. Her entire ensemble was designed to show off this "tummy asset" (for want of a better term that probably doesn't exist in the English language). I don't know if proper etiquette requires that you not stare at a woman's exposed, enlarged stomach when she is suggesting a financial liaison, but I was pretty sure that no book on etiquette dealt with this particular issue. I doubt I was gape-mouthed, but that's the way I felt. In the past, women have reminded me of where their eyes are located when I was otherwise entranced by other parts of their anatomies, but never before or since have I been reminded of the location of a woman's eyes when I was mesmerized by her protruding stomach. But as God is my witness, that occurred.

Although I knew that I wouldn't be able to experience this "experience," a slew of questions began to flow into my brain. I had never had sex with a woman who was pregnant, or more correctly, a woman I knew to be pregnant, and certainly never with someone who was "that" pregnant. I would have remembered. I started wondering what it would be like, how it would work and what the safety requirements would be. I was pretty sure that not even the Kama Sutra covered the position that this form of erotica would require. I also figured that the amount of pre-coital discussion required to accomplish this task would probably sufficiently bore Ebenezer enough to take a powder. However, sexual curiosity is a strong motivator. Luckily, I had the 0500 wake up to fall back on as an excuse.

I chatted with her for a few minutes and paid for her expensive, albeit small, drink. She soon left to seek a more lucrative companion. Jim signaled that we needed to leave.

Back at the BOQ, Jim had duty that night. He made security rounds and then returned to the room. He had strapped on a .45 caliber pistol when we got back from the "club". He took that off and sat it on a table beside his bed. He took off his boots, and since he was on duty, laid on his bunk in his uniform.

I climbed in the other bunk and was soon asleep. And then there was the explosion.

DAY TWO

I WAS BACK AT THE Headquarters of the Chief, Naval Advisory Group as my second day in Vietnam began. I heard one of the officers say that the explosion the night before resulted from an ammunition depot being blown up a few miles away. I couldn't believe it was that far. I never found out if it was one of our depots or one of theirs.

One of our ships was due into port tomorrow afternoon. The officers I was working with had already made the necessary arrangements for me to travel to Vung Tau, where the ship would be tied up. I would travel today to be able to meet the ship tomorrow. The plans were somewhat complicated by the fact that I would be flying late in the afternoon.

To understand the complications begins with the fact that the North Vietnamese had begun an offensive operation a couple of weeks before. It was sort of being used as a test of our new "Vietnamization" strategy. Most of the actual fighting was being done by the ARVN. The U.S. was more or less in a support role. We provided supplies and flew people around, but that was about it. As part of the offensive, a week or so before the Viet Cong had fired some rockets in the area where the ships were located with little effect. They had either been aimed at one of our ships or at the pier that the ship was tied up to. I understood that they didn't even come close, but the result was that Vung Tau was now a combat arena.

To go back a little further, Vung Tau had been, and to a certain extent still was, a resort town on the coast. When the French occupied Indochina, they named it Cap Saint-Jacques and compared it to the French Riviera. I have no idea what the two places had in common — maybe they both had beaches. During the war Vung Tau was used as an in-country R&R locale by the Australian and New Zealand troops that were in Vietnam. It was rumored that the Viet Cong also used it for the same purpose. The net effect of all of this was that there was a "gentleman's agreement" that no fighting would take place in Vung Tau. Although the rocket attack was nowhere near the town and the beaches, the gentleman's agreement had been broken.

Vung Tau was now a combat area, A "Yellow Alert" condition had been put into effect over the region. That translated as something like "enemy personnel had been active in the area and an attack could be imminent." When a Yellow Alert condition was declared, several policies and procedures came into effect. One of which was that a curfew was put in place that required all U.S. military personnel to be inside a military compound from dusk to dawn. Since I was flying in late in the afternoon, it became important that I be conveyed to the military base as soon as I landed.

I was half listening to the discussion going on among the other officers about the preparations that were routinely required and what requirements I had to adhere to. Suddenly, my ears perked up. The discussion had turned to whether I had to "draw a weapon," since I was now traveling to a combat zone. The crux of the discussion centered around whether there was any exception to that requirement which would keep me from having to comply.

My first comment was, "Draw a weapon? We're not talking about my doing a sketch here are we?"

Drawing a weapon suddenly felt a whole lot like I was about to go into combat. I reminded myself that I didn't do combat. The response left more questions than it cleared up.

"You really don't want to draw one if you can avoid it. If you draw one, you have to return it clean. There are only a couple of days a week with a limited number of hours when you can return it and have it inspected. Even if you wrap it in a blanket and never fire it, you will fail the first inspection. You can't leave the country until you pass inspection. You could easily be here another week while you try to turn it in."

Obviously, this didn't sound good. However, my next question, "What happens if I actually need one?" was prompted by the fact that my resume didn't include combat training.

"Don't worry. There are guns everywhere. If you need one, just grab the first one you see."

They came up with the necessary exemption, and I followed their advice.

About 1700 hours I was transported to a different part of the airport where I was to catch the flight to Vung Tau. I was carrying only my briefcase and a small bag with a change of clothes.

The plane I would be flying on was a military chartered flight. The aircraft was a de Havilland DHC-4, commonly known as a Caribou. Since it was often used to carry cargo, it has a ramp at the rear of the plane. The pilots were civilians. I boarded the plane and immediately noticed that the only people on the plane that weren't armed to the teeth, were the two pilots and me. I immediately felt out of place. The soldier sitting next to me, besides having an M-16, had hand grenades hung from his uniform. The fact that I could actually be heading into combat struck me again – and I was going without a weapon.

I looked out the window as we flew. The country was mostly rice paddies with palm trees and thatched huts along the perimeters

17

of the fields. On the ground I noticed a lot of somewhat large, round holes filled with water. My first thought was that they were bomb craters. That conclusion was irrational on several levels – too many, too widespread and in unlikely combat areas. It surprised and concerned me that I was now assuming that everything I saw was somehow related to the war and combat. I made a mental note to try to start seeing things as they were and not filter them through the eyes of war. I made another mental note to ask someone what the holes of water were.

The flight lasted less than an hour. As we landed at Vung Tau I noticed that the sun was beginning to set. Even before the plane had come to a stop, the pilots let down the rear ramp. The soldiers on the plane were streaming off, mostly running down the ramp, and sprinting to jump into trucks parked alongside the tarmac. Having no idea who was supposed to be there to meet me, I exited through the side door and stepped out on the tarmac. I figured I'd be recognized immediately. The trucks loaded quickly and pulled away. Within a minute or two I was standing there by myself. All of the vehicles had left.

There was no one there to meet me.

My first thought, "Oh shit. This is not good."

Luckily my main survival technique, my sense of humor, kicked in. My next thought was, "I don't even see a Holiday Inn. This could be bad."

It was now about 1800 hours. The sun was setting.

The only solution I could come up with was to try to call the detachment from my unit that was temporarily located here to support our ships. I often talked to them over the phone from Guam, so I had a telephone number. They worked out of a warehouse near the pier. The number I had was at the warehouse. I wasn't at all sure that, even if I could find a phone to call them, they would still be there. They ate and slept at a military compound in the area. Their workday normally ended about this time, and they would return to the compound. This was looking worse all the time.

I walked around and found the pilots in a building beside the runway. I asked if they had a phone. They did. Luckily, I had my address book in my briefcase. I looked up the number for the detachment and called it. Someone answered.

Somewhere within the ensuing string of epithets, I managed to convey that I was at the airport. The senior petty officer who answered responded, "Mr. Powell. We heard through the grapevine that you were coming, but no one told us when you'd be here. We're bastard children here. No one tells us anything. I'll be there as soon as I can get there." I told him where I was. "You're lucky that you caught us. We were just leaving."

He told me to wait outside where I was. We needed to get on to the compound as soon as possible.

The heat and humidity only compounded my stress. I looked for a shaded place to sit and wait. There were a lot of buildings and hangars – all closed – a few airplanes, but nowhere that I could sit and get out of the sun. I finally saw a spot where a building offered some shade since the sun was going down behind it. I went and sat on the curb in front of the building and waited. Again, I found myself asking myself what I was doing here. In less than 30 minutes, I saw a gray Navy pickup truck coming down the tarmac. I'm not sure that my feelings were exactly those of the wagon train seeing the cavalry riding over the plains, but they were something like that.

The petty officer who picked me up, Danessen, was a big, machinist mate. He was the senior petty officer among our detachment stationed there and was in charge. Machinist mates are trained to repair diesel engines. He had been transferred to the Squadron Staff from one of the PGs, so he had some experience with Vietnam. That's probably why they sent him to be in charge of our detachment. He wasn't dressed in the army green uniform but was wearing

Navy dungarees. In lieu of a combat helmet he was wearing a hard hat. As I got in the truck, I noted that there was a shotgun and an M-16 perched on the floor between the seats. I had had some time to calm down some. I thanked him for coming, and we pulled away.

As we drove, I half listened to him complaining about the treatment that his guys were receiving. It's not that I doubted it, it was just that I was pretty sure that I really couldn't do anything about it. But maybe I'd have an opportunity to bring it up to someone who could.

We had been driving awhile when Danessen slowed down and pulled to the side of the road. It was now dusk. Not dark, but dark enough that he had turned on the headlights.

He then nodded toward the weapons between the seats and asked, "Mr. Powell, do you know how to use these?"

My response, "Yes. I qualified on small arms. Why?"

"Well sir, the village we are coming up to belongs to Charlie and they have been attacking at dusk. We may have to fight our way through." Charlie was the Viet Cong.

I am here to tell you that there are no words in the English language that will focus your thought processes clearer and quicker than the words, "Fight our way through."

I should add that I quickly analyzed his demeanor to make sure I wasn't getting "tested". I decided he wasn't jerking me around but was simply advising me of a potential problem. People assigned here soon learn to speak in a monotone, even if they are talking about a possible conflict. Shouting is reserved for actual combat.

"Is there any way around?" was my next question. Avoiding a potential conflict seemed like the better solution at this point.

He replied, "No sir. This is the only road."

I reached over and picked up the M-16, tapped the bottom of the clip to make sure it was in, pulled the slide to chamber a round, set it for fully automatic, put the muzzle out the window, and said, "Okay. Let's go."

I was then, and am still, amazed at how calm I was. I was mostly concentrating on making sure that if I started shooting, I was actually shooting at someone who was shooting at me. I didn't want to kill a villager who happened to be holding a hoe. However, there was no doubt in my mind that if I actually saw a villager carrying an AK-47, I would shoot him, or even HER, if I thought she was a combatant. For many years I have gone over in my mind that moment in that village. I have no idea where that calmness and resolution came from. Nothing in my background or training prepared me for that moment, but nonetheless I was calm and sure that I could handle it, if necessary.

I was carefully scanning the area ahead of us as Danessen pulled back on the road. As we drove through the village, I noticed there were children playing and women standing motionless in the doorways to their huts, watching us pass. I didn't see any men. I had no idea whether the lack of men at this time of day was unusual. Maybe they were still in the fields. Maybe they knew that a military truck driving down the road at this time of day represented a danger and they were staying out of sight. On the other hand, maybe we were about to be ambushed. The lack of daylight didn't make things any easier. I scanned the jungle, which was now shades of dark green and black, looking for muzzle flashes from a weapon, since I really wouldn't be able to see anything else.

We were soon through the village and back on the deserted road. I pulled the weapon back in the truck and put it on safety, but I kept it between my legs with the barrel pointed toward the roof. I smiled when I thought that I was actually riding shotgun.

It suddenly hit me that I was actually in a war and that there were actually people here who wanted to kill me. I mentally shrugged.

In a few minutes more, we pulled up to the gate at the compound. The compound was surrounded by tall fences with barbed wire on top. There were searchlights on every corner that lit up the outer perimeter. It reminded me of the photos I'd seen of WWII Concentration Camps.

The guards opened the front gate, and we pulled in. We got out, and they checked the vehicle. We got back in and drove to the main admin building. I got out of the truck and was "greeted" by the officer on duty that night. The fact that he was dressed in a crisply starched and ironed uniform told me all I needed to know about him. I use the term "greeted" loosely, since it became immediately clear that I wasn't welcome. I had no idea what they thought I was there for, but whatever the reason, they had decided that it wasn't for their benefit. I first asked the officer why they hadn't either picked me up or told my people that I was coming so that they could pick me up. The question was brushed off. Then came the clincher.

He said, "We really don't have a place for you to stay here tonight."

After what I had just been through, it was probably wise that I hadn't been issued a side arm.

In my most sarcastic voice, I responded, "Fine. If you'll just endorse my orders and direct me to the nearest hotel, I'll make other arrangements."

I had no idea what he was telling me. He knew, as well as I did, that I had to stay there that night. When I was "escorted" to my room, I found out what he was telling me.

The room had a metal cot with a thin mattress, a chest of drawers and a ceiling fan. Even though the rooms were cleaned by Vietnamese maids, it was clear that the room hadn't been cleaned recently – possibly ever. There was sand and dirt on the floor and mosquitoes on the ceiling and walls, a bag that enclosed the mattress, but nothing else. The rooms for those officers who were permanently assigned were air conditioned and cleaned daily.

When I turned on the ceiling fan, it stirred up the sand and dirt, but it kept the mosquitoes off me. When I turned the fan off, the mosquitoes attacked. I spent the night alternating between turning the fan off and on. The sleeping that I did, I did in my uniform using my briefcase as a pillow.

As uncomfortable as I was, I lay there and thought of Sarah. I continued to go over that morning in my mind. That experience really didn't make sense, but it made far more sense than what I found myself involved in now. In some inexplicable way, she was making everything bearable.

The next morning, I got up to go to the head to take a shower. No one spoke to me. I hadn't brought a towel, so I dried off with paper towels.

The message came across loud and clear.

If they were concerned that I was here on some kind of inspection tour, they now had reason to be concerned. I was already composing my report in my head.

Military Moron Rule Number 6: If you are being inspected and have something you don't want the inspector to find, make sure you make him feel uncomfortable on the off chance that he's not any smarter than you are, and he'll just go away.

DAY THREE

AFTER MY SHOWER, I WALKED over to the officers' mess for breakfast. I walked through the chow line, served myself, found a vacant seat and ate in silence. I wasn't invited to join any of the other people in the room, which was okay since I really wasn't in a mood to talk, anyway.

The first item on my agenda for the day was to report to the area commander that the ships reported to when they were in the river. Since the ships were under their command when they were in port, technically the logistics matters that I had been sent to assist with were their responsibility. If anyone should have been concerned about my being on some kind of inspection tour, these were the guys. I think that the officer who greeted me the night before was actually assigned there. After what I had been through, I wasn't looking forward to this visit.

The ship wasn't due in until later that day. I would be staying aboard the ship for the remainder of my time in Vung Tau, which was a relief. Also, the message traffic that I had read in Guam indicated that the ships appreciated my coming. The bad news – I was in a combat zone and I had no idea what I would accomplish, if anything.

One of the sailors who was part of the squadron detachment serving at the pier had been assigned by Danessen to drive me. I found him waiting outside. Armed with my briefcase and my clothes bag, since I would be moving aboard ship later that day, we headed off to whatever subtle, or possibly not so subtle, interrogation I was about to encounter.

We drove to another nondescript office building. I walked in and introduced myself and was told that the officer-in-charge wanted to see me. That was routine. I found a chair and sat and waited. After some time, I was shown into the office of the Commander.

The Commanding Officer was a senior Navy commander. As I entered his office, he stood, came around from behind his desk and stuck his hand out to shake mine. He was probably in his 30s, of mid height and weight and sported a burr haircut. I could see from the stuff on his wall that he had spent most of his time at sea and had been the captain of at least one ship. His main responsibility was to oversee the operation of the "Swift Boats" that operated in this area. Swift Boats were small, armed patrol boats that operated in the rivers. They were later introduced to the public in the movie "Apocalypse Now" and in a Presidential campaign. After a few minutes of obligatory pleasantries, where he asked about my trip and the accommodations – to which my response was simply "fine" - we got down to business. The first question out of his mouth was, "Why are you here?"

I briefly explained that the ships were having problems getting resupplied and I had been sent to see if there was anything I could do to attempt to resolve the problem. Although resupply was really the responsibility of the Army, problems with resupply would be within the purview of this command to resolve. His demeanor quickly changed to one of why someone thought that he wasn't doing his job. He wanted specifics. I had them.

Most of the problems revolved around the fact that the ships only pulled into port for a few days. The ships sent messages ahead with their order for resupply. The messages were addressed to the Army Depot which was responsible for filling the order, but several others, including me and the command were copied on the messages. The ships expected to find the orders filled and on the pier when they pulled into port. The orders weren't on the pier when they came in and when they finally received what they had ordered, it often didn't include much of what was on the requisition. As far as I could tell the Army started filling the order when the ship arrived, which didn't allow sufficient time to obtain any items which weren't in stock.

I started getting the standard excuses – the ships weren't the primary duty of this command, they were busy and understaffed, etc., etc.

I decided to cut this meeting short and possibly salvage what was quickly going south.

"Commander. Neither my CO nor I are holding you responsible. If anything, this is an Army fuck up. These ships are my primary responsibility. I was trained to speak Supply, and I'm familiar with what the procedures are supposed to be. That's why I was sent here. Now, if you and I can get on the same side on this thing, possibly, although I have my doubts, I can assist with resolving the problem. That would help both of us. I am going to need to file a report. I would like it to read that you and I worked together to get this thing resolved."

Normally, that level of candidness would have been considered out of line, but I had been on Guam for a couple of years and would be there for at least another year and a half. I was now in Vietnam. Both of my jobs had been ashore rather than at sea. I didn't intend to make the Navy a career, but even if I were going to, having the jobs I had been in for the time I was in them had probably already taken its toll on that notion. Ruining my "career" was no longer an option. Sending me to Guam for over three years wasn't an option. And I couldn't be sent to Vietnam, since I was already here. The standard hand slaps were no longer available.

His demeanor changed immediately. He stood, stuck out his hand, and said, "Sounds good to me. If I can be of any help, let me know." I think we were both relieved.

Next stop was the Army Depot.

On the way, my driver updated me on the status. The Army was reducing the size of its presence in this area, which included reducing the size of its supply staff. People were getting reassigned.

We pulled up to the Depot and I walked inside. I was met with what could only be described as "chaos". There was a receiving counter where soldiers were lined up two deep and shouting. There was a single soldier on the other side trying, mostly unsuccessfully, to deal with the situation.

I turned to my driver and asked if there was anyone that they normally dealt with. His response, "Well we normally worked with Sergeant May, but he was transferred last week."

Great. SNAFU! I pulled rank and moved up to the counter. I addressed the soldier behind the counter. "I need to speak to the Officer-in-Charge."

"He's not here, sir. He doesn't really work here so he rarely comes over here."

"Okay, so who is in charge here?' (I was assuming someone was in charge.)

"Staff Sergeant Rollins, sir. But he's not here right now either. I wish he was."

"So, when do you expect him back?"

"Well I don't really know sir. He left about an hour ago and said he'd be back later."

"Tell him I'll be back after lunch and I want to talk to him."

"Yes sir. If you don't mind sir, I need to get back to work."

"Carry on."

As we walked back to the truck, I said to no one in particular, "Supply is probably the least of their problems."

By the time we got back to the pier, the ship, the U.S.S. Seattle, had pulled in. The Seattle's Commanding Officer, Sam King, yelled from the bridge, "Powell, I heard you were coming over here, but I thought even a Supply Officer couldn't be that stupid. Wait there, I'll come down, and we'll go to lunch."

I dropped off my stuff with the quarterdeck and asked them to put it in my stateroom. The duty petty officer on the quarterdeck told me that I was bunking with the captain. In case this sounds plush, the captain has his own stateroom aboard ship, which on a PG is about the size of a medium-sized, walk-in closet. There is a bunk installed above his bed for guests. Sam came down dressed in shorts and a T-shirt. He and I knew each other from Guam and had gone drinking a couple of times. We got in the jeep reserved for the ship and headed off. The first topic was where we were going to lunch.

"I know a really good restaurant in town. The fare is mostly seafood cooked Vung Tau style. The clientele is Vietnamese with a few round eyes. Vung Tau is an in-country R&R location for the Aussies and Kiwis and reportedly for the Viet Cong. So, there is an unwritten agreement that it's neutral. It never gets attacked. Maybe you'll get to meet some real Viet Cong."

I assumed he was kidding about the last comment, but I wasn't sure.

We found a table and ordered the crab and a couple of beers.

He began the with, "Well tell me about what's going on on Guam these days."

I responded, "Pretty much the same as what was going on when you left. No one seems to have much of an idea what's really happening. No one makes any plans much past next week."

That wasn't what he was asking.

He then got to the point. "I hear that you and your wife are splitting up." That was true. How he knew about it was the surprise.

"Yeah, she got fed up with me and the island about the same time. She really didn't like living on Guam. The last straw was when she found out that we'd be on the island another year and a half. We weren't doing too well before then. I also pretty much decided that she was fooling around with one of the guys she was working with. None of it came as a big surprise to me."

I took a sip of my beer. "How the hell did you know that anyway? I thought I was kind of keeping it quiet."

His response, "The grapevine … scuttlebutt."

"Yeah, I know about the grapevine. Sometimes it seems like all you guys are doing over here is sitting around gossiping like a bunch of old women. By the way, the grapevine normally gets its wrong." I took another sip. "I guess in my case it was true. Sort of like a stopped clock. It's right twice a day."

"Is she staying on Guam?"

"Oh hell no. She's ready to leave as soon as the arrangements are finalized. She's due to fly out in a few weeks."

We paused when they brought the food and we started to eat. The crab was really good.

After a minute Sam asked, "Has it been difficult?"

"Not sure what you mean? Do you mean breaking up? No, not really."

"No, I really mean getting her flown back to the states."

"That part has been difficult. I had no idea where to start to make the arrangements to ship her out. Not only was there getting her a flight back to the states, but as you know we're living in base housing. I have to give it up after she leaves. So, I had to arrange a move out of housing and a shipment of her stuff home as well as arranging her a flight off the island."

"How'd you get all that done? I mean how did you know where to go and who to talk to?"

"Well, when it was clear that we were splitting and she was going back to the States, I stayed at the office late one night and went in to talk to the CSO and explained the problem. He was great. He made a couple of calls the next day and got me a contact. I met with the woman and got a checklist of the things I had to accomplish. I guess the hardest part was that I had to write a letter explaining the reason for her leaving early. Putting that down on paper knowing that it would become part of my record ... well, suffice it to say, it wasn't easy. I worked on that letter for several hours."

"Are you still in housing?"

"Yeah." I took a bite and grinned while I chewed. "She wanted me to move onto the couch until she left. I told her that she was living there because of me. The house was issued to me. If she wanted one of us to sleep on the couch, it was going to be her."

He laughed. "I'm sure that went over well. Did she move to the couch?"

"Sort of. We still shared the bed occasionally. I sometimes fell asleep on the couch after an evening at the club. She recently moved out, anyway."

We both got quiet again and ate.

I then asked, "You seem more than casually interested in this. Is there a reason?"

He paused and then answered, "My wife hates Guam and wants to go home. I may need to call on you to get directions on how to ship her out. The idea of having to write a letter stating that we're splitting up ..." He trailed off, but I understood.

"Come see me when you get back to Guam. I have a file of forms and letters made up. I'll give you copies."

We changed the subject and started discussing what the ships were doing and the problems they were having getting supplied.

In a few minutes he interrupted and said, "I hope I'm not prying, but what happened to her and the guy you think she was banging?"

"That poor bastard. His wife found out about their affair and ended his marriage. After that the bitch dumped him too. He's actually a good guy. He and I were diving buddies. Spent some good times together. I'll miss him a lot more than I'll miss her."

"So, she was actually screwing him?"

"I guess so. I never really asked. I try to avoid asking questions when I don 't know how I'm going to handle the answer. But there was pretty strong circumstantial evidence."

"The grapevine has a lot more of the wives screwing around. Any of that true?"

I knew it was true, but I wasn't going to make things worse. Besides, his wife was one of them.

"Well, since very few of the wives have jobs, and most are putting off having children until they are back in the States, most of them are bored stiff. I do run into flocks of them occasionally at happy hour. Usually sitting and drinking with some of the bachelors. It wouldn't surprise me if they were, but I don't have any 'first-hand knowledge,' so all I'd being doing is speculating and spreading rumors. There's plenty enough of that already."

"You probably know that your name comes up in those discussions."

"I wish I could say that I was surprised, but knowing the way you girls gossip, I'm not. I guess I should I be flattered. I don't really think of myself as being in the good-looking, stud category. But truthfully, as horny as we all get on Guam ... I hope I'm smart enough not to shit where I eat. I have all the problems I can handle right now."

Actually, one part of that was true. I was having an affair, but not with anyone he would know.

We finished lunch. I insisted on paying, since I could include it on my expense report, and we left.

As we walked out, I asked, "Hey, I'm supposed to meet the Sergeant in Charge of the Army supply operation this afternoon. Could you run me by the warehouse? If you're not doing anything, it would probably be good if you sat in on that meeting. You can give more specifics than I can."

He agreed and we drove to the Army Depot.

When I got there, not much had changed. The crowd in front of the counter was smaller, and now there were two guys working it, but it was still chaos – just slightly reduced chaos. The guy I talked to earlier saw me and said, "Sergeant Rollins asked if he could meet with you in the morning. He wants the officer-in-charge to be in on the meeting."

I didn't have much of an alternative, so I agreed.

The Captain had to meet with the commander I had met with earlier that morning, so he dropped me off at the ship and drove off. As he was leaving, I suggested that he might want to put on a clean uniform. His response was, "Why?" A one-word question and answer.

Later that afternoon, approaching sundown, the weather was cooler, and it was quiet. I walked to the stern of the ship to sit outside and begin to work on my report. I needed to make notes on what had occurred that day. I looked up to see an Army sentry walking the pier. I briefly recalled the admonition that only a couple of weeks before this pier was the target of a rocket attack about this time of day. I thought for a moment if there was something I should do to be a little safer. I quickly reviewed options – go back inside the ship, go sit on the shore ... I decided that each option had its own risks. Ah well, you pay your money ...

I found a quiet place to sit on the fantail. At that time of day, it was shaded by the trees on the shore. As I sat down, three Huey helicopters came flying over headed toward the Army Base. Before I saw them, I could hear them – nothing else sounds like the whop, whop, whop of Hueys. That sound will always be associated with Vietnam. I then noticed a "roach" on the deck. For those of you who didn't grow up in the sixties, it wasn't a bug. I picked it up and tossed it overboard. These days marijuana was everywhere.

The military draft was still in effect, so much of the officer corps was made up of individuals coming right out of college who chose a commission as an officer rather than risk the uncertainty that getting drafted would entail. The result was that in many ways it was the kind of Navy that a democracy should strive for. The first duty station I went to on active duty was the Navy Supply Corps School located in Athens, Georgia where I was trained to be a Supply Officer. I assume it was put there because of the influence of one of the powerful Georgia senators. When I stood in line for formation in the morning, the guy who stood on my left had a master's degree in architecture from Yale and the guy on my right had a degree in religion from Princeton. My platoon was rife with individuals who held MBAs.

A few weeks before we reported to the school, most of us were still in college where sex, drugs and rock and roll held sway. The idea that this was all going to change with a "swearing in" ceremony was naïve, at best. People smoking weed at the school were almost as common as those drinking beer. The situation in the rest of the Navy wasn't much different. I don't want to suggest that the entire Navy officer corps was made up of these kinds of individuals, nor do I want to suggest that most of the officers were smoking dope, but they were certainly more tolerant of those who did. Naturally, many of the officers were graduates of the Naval Academy. Most of the Academy graduates and a small group who wanted to make the Navy a career believed that the officers from college were all hippies and that their lifestyle was anathema to a well-run military organization. They were generally referred to by the rest of us as "lifers" if they hadn't gone to the Naval Academy, or "boat schoolers" if they had.

As I sat there thinking about the difference between those of us who had just come from college and the Academy graduates, I recalled a recent incident.

I was sitting in the officers' club on Guam drinking with several of the junior officers who were assigned to the PGs. The topic of conversation was about life aboard a PG. One of the officers said that first thing every morning, "I walk around the deck, picking up the roaches and throwing them overboard. The Old Man goes ballistic if he finds these." One of the boat schoolers chimed in, "I know what you're talking about. We have used every kind of bug spray we can find, but we just can't seem to get rid of the damn roaches." A pregnant silence fell over the group. I looked around and most of the group were looking into their beers trying to stifle a grin. The subject was quickly changed.

My mind returned to trying to make some notes, but thoughts of Sarah kept intruding. Suddenly from behind me the solitude was shattered by a loud explosion. I spun around. A shaft of water erupted from the river. My first thought was that the ship was being rocketed or the enemy had set off a mine. I would have seen or heard the rocket, so it was more likely a mine. Vietnamese swimmers, known as "sappers," were known to attach mines to the hulls of Navy ships.

I leapt up and, for the second time in a couple of days, I didn't know exactly how I should react. Sappers usually attacked at night. I froze. I looked over at the sentry to see how he was reacting. He was standing there totally unmoved. He was looking at the water, but still had his rifle slung over his shoulder. An explosion – a sentry doing nothing. Maybe he didn't know how to react, but not even unshouldering his weapon? It didn't make sense. Then it came to me. The sentry had thrown a hand grenade in the water. More to the point, he had thrown a percussion grenade in the water.

The purpose of percussion grenades was to kill any sappers in the water. Throwing one in the water now was simply to discourage sappers from trying to mine the ship. His face was hidden from me, but I knew he was smiling. Tossing it in the water without warning me was a grand joke. As I felt my heartbeat beginning to return to normal, I again thought that it was probably a good idea that I hadn't been issued a weapon. My firing off a few rounds would probably have spoiled the joke.

During the night, the sentry on duty on the pier continued to periodically toss percussion grenades in the water. From inside the ship, the explosion was muffled and would wake me, to be followed by a loud clang, as the underwater percussion wave hit the side of the ship. After the first one, I had learned to lay still. The ceiling above my bunk was less than two feet away. I'd probably have a bruise on my head resulting from my jerking up when the first one went off. As I lay awake in my bunk, I decided that this was still better than another night of fighting sand and mosquitoes. At least it was air conditioned. The captain wasn't aboard. I assume he had an air-conditioned room at the compound.

I decided that thinking about something else might allow me to sleep. I tried to concentrate on my report, but Sarah kept interrupting my thoughts. In a duel between sex and boring, sex will win every time. I closed my eyes and surrendered to the memories.

My mind took me to the last time we were together. Her mother was visiting, and Sarah had invited me over for dinner to meet her mother and to see the base house that she and her husband had just moved into. Odd that I didn't think much about that at the time.

Sarah's husband was still out of town.

I tried to be on my best behavior. I came from work, so I was still in uniform. Sarah met me at the door with a gin and tonic. I sat and talked to her mother while Sarah finished setting the table. It was the best meal I had had in a long time. By the end of the meal, the gin and the wine had begun to take its toll.

While Sarah cleaned the table, her mother and I went into the living room. She sat on the couch, and I sat in the only chair, which was across the room. A little too far for casual conversation. I tried to recall what we talked about. I think we chatted about what I did. She knew about Barbie and my split up and inquired how I was doing. When Sarah joined us, my southern gentleman training kicked in, and I rose and insisted that she take the chair. I grabbed a pillow cushion and moved to sit on the floor between them. I recall trying to steer the conversation toward her mother. She was almost as charming as her daughter.

I don't recall staying much longer, however, by the end of the evening I was lying on the floor propped up on one arm. Possibly it was the booze that made this seem so not out of the ordinary. At about 9:00, I rose, offered my thanks for the home-cooked meal and told her mother how much I enjoyed meeting her – and left.

When I spoke to Sarah on the phone the next day, she told me that she had asked her mother what she thought about me. She said that her mother's only comment was, "I know why your husband doesn't want him over here when he's not home."

I drifted to sleep pondering the many questions which that raised. I was only sure of one thing – I was falling for Sarah.

SARAH

OUR RELATIONSHIP HAD STARTED A few weeks before. At the time Barbie, my future ex-wife, whom I had started referring to as the Wicked Bitch of the East shortened to the East Bitch or EB, had temporarily moved out. I was living in the house by myself. I had no idea if she intended to move back to the house since she wasn't due to fly out of Guam for a few weeks. I really hoped she wouldn't. I'd had enough.

Sarah and her husband were babysitting a house down the street while the couple who actually lived there was temporarily back in the States. Sarah's husband was in the Air Force and was also away from Guam on some temporary assignment. Sarah and Barbie had become friends and would occasionally get together for coffee in the morning. EB had quit her job.

I really didn't know where she was, but I had the telephone number of a friend of hers I could call if I really needed to get in touch with her. The empty house had gotten to me that morning. I was beginning to realize what my life was going to be for the next year and three months. I still hadn't told my parents. I wasn't looking forward to that. I didn't know if she had told hers. Also, at the time there were over 6,000 unaccompanied military personnel on the island and about 20 single women – teachers, nurses and a few single, female officers. My chances for female companionship for the rest of my time on the island were virtually nil. Then there was the divorce itself. I knew I didn't want to get back together, but I also couldn't figure out where the hell it had all gone wrong.

I had the duty the night before. On a duty night, you were required to sleep at the office. However, after the morning meeting the next day, you were authorized to take some time to go home, shower, put on a clean uniform and eat breakfast. I had been home for a few minutes when there was a knock at the kitchen door. It was Sarah.

I found Sarah attractive. She was blonde and slightly overweight with large boobs. The kind of body that one can almost sink into. She had a great smile and a wonderful sense of humor. Although I tried to hide from her the fact that I was attracted to her, I found out later she knew. She had recently had a baby who was asleep in the carrier that she had with her.

She began by asking if Barbie was here.

"Well, actually she's not. Frankly, I'm not real sure if she's coming back. Uh … to be honest, we're splitting up."

"Yes, she told me that. I'm very sorry."

"I just made some coffee. Would you like to come in and have a cup? We Supply Officers know how to make coffee." Lame I know, but it was all that I could come up with at the moment.

"Sure. Layla's asleep. I have some time. I'll put her on the couch."

I poured the coffee and we sat at the kitchen table.

"So, how are you holding up?"

Any other time, I probably would have responded with, "Fine." But instead I started talking. As I talked, the whole story came out. Normally, I would have been mortified that I had related the whole sordid tale, but as Sarah just sat there and listened, I felt okay finally being able to tell someone.

When I finished, she just said, "You've been through a lot. I am really sorry."

I mumbled my appreciation and started to apologize for dumping all of this on her, but she interrupted and said, "Listen, I need to get back home. I don't want to leave you here like this. Get your uniform and come to my house. You can shower there, and I'll make you some breakfast." Having someone take over right then was relieving.

In a few minutes I knocked on her door. She opened it and said, "I'm drawing you a bath in the upstairs bathroom. I'm making some breakfast."

I went upstairs and found the bath water running. I turned off the water, got undressed and got in the tub. The warm water was relaxing.

I had been lying there for a few minutes, when I heard the door to the bathroom open. I turned and it was Sarah dressed in a silky kimono carrying a couple of bath towels. Before I said anything, she said, "I'm going to wash your hair. Slide forward." She untied the sash and let the kimono drop on the floor and laid the towels on the floor beside the tub. Her nude body was as lovely and sexy as I had imagined. Without saying another word, I inched forward and she got in the tub behind me. She stretched out her legs on both sides of me. My arousal was apparent.

She reached for a pitcher on the side of the tub, filled it with warm water and pulled me back against her chest. She told me to close my eyes and poured the warm water over my hair, smoothing it back as she poured. She then reached for the shampoo, poured a small amount in her hand and started rubbing it through my hair. Once the shampoo had filled my hair, she started massaging my scalp. I could not recall having experience anything more sensual before then – or possibly since.

I started to stammer some kind of appreciation. She just said, "Hush. Enjoy this. You deserve it."

"Stay there a minute." She got out of the tub and picked up a towel and dried herself. Watching a woman dry herself can only be described as visual poetry. She wrapped the towel around her and then picked up the other towel and held it open for me. She wrapped me in it and dried me off.

"Leave it on the floor." I dropped it. Without saying another word, she took my head in her hands and kissed me passionately. She then looked in my eyes and said, "You really need this." Taking my hand, she led me into the bedroom.

We made romantic, passionate love. When we were both spent, lying on the bed facing each other, I said the first thing I had said. "Will this continue or was this the only time?" Her response was, "That was absolutely wonderful, and God I hope this will continue."

It's hard to explain, but in a way, she probably saved my life.

DAY FOUR

It's AMAZING WHAT ONE CAN get used to. After a night of being periodically awakened by percussion grenades, I awoke early the next morning. I immediately started thinking about my upcoming meeting with the Army. My entire reason for being in Vietnam probably hinged on the outcome of that meeting, and I had no agenda. I really wasn't sure what I was going to ask for. Asking, "Can you do better?" seemed lame, at best. Ah well, I'd wing it.

I got up, shaved, brushed my teeth and put back on the same uniform I'd been wearing for the last two days. The ship wasn't hooked up to shore water so unnecessary use of water was out. No shower. I went to the officers' dining room, which in the Navy is known as the Wardroom. This room was only slightly larger than the Captain's stateroom. It consisted of a small table with benches on two sides and a chair on a third. It would seat about five individuals, uncomfortably. However, since there were only four officers assigned to the ship in total, including the captain, it was adequate. I poured a cup of coffee and sat down at the table.

I was the first person there. A clipboard lay on the table with the messages that had come in overnight. I picked it up and started thumbing through. If there was anything intended for me, it would be sent to the ship. It was also a way for me to keep abreast of what was going on.

After a few minutes the Executive Officer, Rick, came in. Another officer I knew from Guam. He greeted me, and grinning asked, "How'd you sleep?' I could truthfully reply, "Better than at the compound."

He poured some coffee and sat down. The cook's assistant came over and asked what we'd like for breakfast … and then told us the somewhat limited options. We ordered and Rick asked, "So what's on your schedule today?"

"I can tell you where I'm going. I can also tell you who I'm going to meet with, but damned if I know if I'm going to accomplish anything."

"What's the problem?"

"Well, I can tell you from the book how everything is supposed to work. Rarely does it really work that way. In this business, contacts are everything. The way that people are getting reassigned, the contact that you set up today may be gone in a week, and you're back at square one. On top of that, I'm supposed to fly back to Saigon this afternoon. I don't have a lot of time."

"Did they tell you that they may be pulling our ships out in a month or so? They're planning to turn things over to the South Vietnamese."

Currently, we had five ships. Two or three at a time were assigned to Vietnam duty. They would patrol the coast for a couple of weeks, pull into port to get resupplied, sail back to a harbor at an island off the coast of Vietnam and trade off with one of the other ships on standby. The new ship would repeat the process.

The area the ships patrolled was the southern sector of the country. The job was to look for boats and ships carrying military contraband. The dirty little secret was that most of the contraband came in via the Ho Chi Minh Trail. Any ships that they might have encountered that were actually carrying contraband knew the area that our ships patrolled and stayed north of that. At best, the ships were a deterrent.

I did some quick mental calculations. If the information he provided was valid, a ship was on patrol for two weeks, in port for a few days and back to the island, so they were normally out for about three weeks. Two ships – six weeks. A total of two resupplies. I was here to try to fix something that might occur only twice. The good news was that even if I couldn't fix it, it probably didn't make much difference. The bad news … well the bad news was that I was over here trying to fix it.

This war was getting weirder by the minute.

I went up on the deck and met Petty Officer Castro, a Filipino, who was the Storekeeper for the ship. He was in charge of ordering, receiving, storing and issuing parts that were onboard ship and ordering replacements or any other parts that weren't stored aboard ship. The Captain had agreed to allow him to drive me over to the Army Depot again today.

We arrived, and we both went inside. It all seemed to be a replay of the day before. Two guys behind the counter. People yelling. I got the attention of the soldier behind the counter. He told me that the First Sergeant was in the back. He nodded in the direction and seemed to smirk.

I walked past the counter and through a valley of shelves and stacks of material. I found the desk with the First Sergeant sitting behind it with his feet propped up on the desk. He saw I was an officer and quickly jumped to his feet and started pulling a tarp down over the cases behind him. He stuttered, "Are you … uh … Lieutenant Powell?" I said I was and asked about the officer in charge.

"Sorry sir." He still seemed nervous. "He got called away this morning and won't be meeting with us. He told me to meet with you and see if there was anything we can do to help the Navy. Before we start, would you like a drink?"

It was then I noticed that surrounding his desk were cases of booze, cigarettes, even cigars. He had managed to pull the tarp over only one of the stacks.

I declined the drink.

"Well, can I interest you in a fifth of good scotch or a box of Cuban cigars? On the house."

I had heard the rumors about these guys, but I had rejected them out of hand. The guys that were running these kinds of operations were reputed to be going back to the States with a large wad of cash. Normally, this would have just irritated me, and I would have looked the other way. But I was obviously being bribed. That grabbed my attention. The fact that the officer in charge of this operation was conveniently absent reinforced my suspicions.

"Thanks anyway, but I've got a plane to catch back to Saigon this afternoon, and I need to see if I can get some things straightened out."

"Sure boss, what's the problem?"

"As you know, I work with the PGs. They are having problems getting supplied here, and I was sent over here from Guam to look into it and see if there was something I could do to straighten things out."

"You say that they are having problems getting supplied. That's the first I've heard of it. Like what kind of problems?"

I could feel Castro grimace since he knew that was a lie. On the other hand, this guy seemed so detached from this operation that maybe it was the first he had heard of it.

"Well, they only pull in here for a couple of days to resupply. They send a requisition ahead by message with what they need. I have some guys working for me over here who are supposed to pick up the order a few days before the ship gets here. They're supposed go through what's issued to make sure everything that the ship ordered is there, and have the stuff waiting on the pier when the ship comes in. If something is missing, they have some time to get back to you and see if the missing items can be located or can be gotten from somewhere else before the ship has to leave."

I paused to decide exactly how I wanted to tell him that none of that was working as it was supposed to, and it was because he wasn't doing his job. I assumed that because of his rank that I didn't need to tell him that if a piece of critical equipment was inoperable for lack of a necessary part and because of his screwed up operation the part wasn't going to be there when the ship left, that people began to get cranky. Even though I knew immediately that this guy really could have cared less, I really didn't want to piss him off since I would probably need his cooperation to resolve the problem.

So, I continued as if I was simply explaining what the problem was. "The way it's actually working is that the order is filled on the day that the ship arrives. By the time it gets to the ship, if there are things missing, it's too late. Food is one problem, but the real problem is that if there are parts that they need that aren't on the pier when they get here, the chances of getting them are pretty much nil."

He looked down and rifled through some papers on his desk considering his answer. Then looked up and said, "Lieutenant, let me level with you. As you know this is an Army base. Our principal job is to supply the Army. These ships got dumped on us, and we don't know shit about supplying ships. On top of that, you've seen what goes on out front. We're badly understaffed, and they aren't going to send us any more help. If I don't make the Army my top priority, I'm going to have some bird colonel down here eating a hole in my trousers. What would you do in my situation?"

No wonder the officer in charge of this place had bailed on the meeting. I was earlier concerned that this was exactly what I was going to find, but truthfully, I understood his predicament. I had considered this and had only come up with one possible solution.

"Okay sergeant, your problem is manpower. I have some people. Let's figure out a way that they can fill the orders for the ships."

"Sir, you know that there's a whole book of Army regulations that your idea would violate."

"Yeah, I do know that, but ..." as I looked behind him, "you don't seem overly concerned about regulations." I paused for effect. "Also, I think there's a way that we can do this more or less legally."

"I'm listening."

"It's not unusual for some activities in the States to operate like a Sears. The customers pull what they need and check out with one of your guys. They'll need to learn your system for locating the stuff. That shouldn't take long. They can come over to pull our stuff after you normally secure, so they won't be in your way. You'll need to detail a guy to be here to assist in finding things and to check them out when they're finished. Your guy will handle the paperwork, my guys will be the labor to pull it. There are some details that will need to be worked out – like your guy needs a copy of the message from the ship to compare against what my guys actually pull. Also, they don't bring in any personal bags, and they turn their pockets inside out while they're here – but those things can be worked out." I hoped he realized that that last part was a semi-joke, but he obviously missed it.

"That might work. Let me think about it and I'll get back to you."

"If you want to try this, you have exactly one hour to make your decision. I'm catching a plane back to Saigon this afternoon. If you want to try it, I'll let my people know. If I don't hear back from you, then I will assume it's a no go, and that's what I'll take back ... and will be in my report. Call me at the ship."

I could tell he was shaken, but I also knew that he thought it might work.

Petty Officer Castro, who was sitting there during the meeting, then spoke up. "Our guys already know where most of the stuff is stored. I could train them how to use the locator system. This could work."

I thanked the sergeant for his time and got up to leave, reminding him he had one hour to decide.

We walked through the crowd, got in the truck and drove back to the ship.

Castro was quiet for a minute then said, "That's a good idea. Our guys really don't have a lot to do when the ships aren't in port. I'm sort of looking forward to telling them that they are going to become 'Supply Pukes.'"

We were back at the ship before the noon meal. I decided to do some public relations work and visit the cook. Food service was also a function that was within my bailiwick.

The PGs had a ship's complement of four officers and 20 enlisted men. On a larger ship, the officers had their own cooks. Since this ship was so small, the cook, with one assistant, prepared the meals for everyone on the ship. They worked out of a galley that was hardly larger than a household kitchen. The equipment was also similar – a four burner stove, a refrigerator and a dishwasher. A freezer and a storeroom were also provided, but were located in another part of the ship. I never ceased to be amazed that they could prepare three meals a day for 24 people … one of whom was the ship's captain.

At sea, good food aboard ship is critical. It is often the high point of a day. Bad food causes morale problems. Because of that, the Navy pays a lot of attention to food preparation. The cooks that were sent to PGs were some of the best that the Navy had.

I caught the cook between breakfast and lunch. He was sitting at a table drinking coffee and reading a paperback.

Before he saw me, I yelled across the room, "Well they haven't thrown you overboard yet. You obviously are doing something right."

Petty Officer Thomas looked up and struggled up from behind the table. "Lieutenant Powell! John told me you were at breakfast this morning. What are you doing over here?"

I chuckled. "Well, I'm not real sure, but I'll let you know when I find out. What's for lunch?"

"I'm doing baked chicken with mashed potatoes and peas, along with a green salad."

"That doesn't sound too bad. What's for dessert?

"Since we're in port I can serve ice cream. Saves me from having to bake."

"The word I'm getting in Guam is that you're having problems getting your orders filled from the Army. What's the straight skinny?"

"Well that's pretty much true. I get about two-thirds of what I order. It normally comes the day after we arrive. I have to go through what we get, compare that to what I ordered, bounce that against my menus and start making changes. I generally make a trip over to the warehouse to see what they do have and process a high-priority requisition for the stuff they have in stock. That usually irritates them, but the Old Man backs me up. Makes for some weird meals, though."

"I'll bet. I'm working on trying to get our guys to be able to pull our orders ahead of time, so that they can let you know what's not there before you pull into port."

"That would make a big difference if you could accomplish that. Do you think you can do it?"

"Beats me. I'm dealing with the Army, and they aren't overly sympathetic to the Navy's problems. But I'll let you know. I'll be back for lunch. Don't do anything special for me. Lobster and baked potato would be plenty enough."

He laughed.

"Right now, I need to meet with our guys at the warehouse. I'll try to be back for lunch. However, I also need to go back and talk to the Commander about what I'm trying to do and get his support. And I'm supposed to fly back to Saigon this afternoon. So if I don't make lunch, it really doesn't have anything to do with what I've heard about your burnt chicken and lumpy mashed potatoes."

He grinned. "Thanks for stopping by and especially for anything you can do to straighten out our resupply problem."

"No sweat. Good seeing you."

I looked at my watch. It had been about 30 minutes since I'd left the warehouse.

I left the ship and walked over to our warehouse beside the pier. I looked for Danessen. I found him working on a piece of machinery.

"Hey Danessen."

He put down the wrench in his hands, grabbed a rag and started to wipe the grease off his hands. Before he had gotten it all off, he stuck out his hand to shake mine. I of course shook it. I could clean my hand later.

"How's it going sir? I heard you met with the Army this morning."

"Yeah. It went a little better than I had expected, but they made it clear that we aren't one of their priorities. I suggested to the First Sergeant that maybe you guys could pull the stuff for the ships. With some training and help from one of their guys, I think you guys could knock it out in a couple of hours. It should make a big difference if I can pull this off."

"We'd be more than willing to do that sir, but all the other stuff we have to do for the Army could complicate things."

"I thought about that. If I get a go ahead from the Army, I plan to go back to see the Commander and see if he can do anything about making sure that this is a priority when you guys are being assigned extra duty. They're supposed to get back to me in the next few minutes and let me know if they're onboard. My problem is I'm running out of time. I'm supposed to fly back to Saigon this afternoon. Which reminds me. I need to talk to the Commander about all of this. Could you have one of your guys run me over there?"

"Sure. I'll take you."

We walked out and got in the truck. Then I remembered. "Wait a minute."

I jumped out and jogged back to the ship. I stood at the bottom of the brow (the gangplank) and shouted to the sailor on watch. "I'm expecting a call from the Army. If it comes in just take a message. If they want to talk to me, have them call me over at headquarters." I thought for a minute. I really didn't recognize the sailor. "You do know who I am don't you?"

"Yessir. You're Lieutenant Powell from the staff."

"And you understand what I need you to do?"

"Yessir."

There was actually a pretty good chance that was true.

We then drove to the Command Headquarters. We walked in. I asked the duty petty officer if the Commander was in and available. "Tell him it's Lieutenant Powell."

"Yes sir. I'll see." He went in the back, came back and said, "He'll see you sir."

I told Danessen to wait for me, that I wouldn't be long.

I walked into the Commander's office. He was waiting in front of his desk and we shook hands. We both sat in the chairs in front of his desk.

He began, "So have you resolved this thing?"

I responded, "Maybe."

I then explained what I had proposed and where we were.

He thought a moment and said, "Sounds like it might work. When will you know if the Army's onboard?"

I told him I was waiting for the call.

"Do you need my help with anything?"

"Yes, sir. Just one thing. I need to make sure that my guys are available to go pull the stuff. Which means that they can't be assigned other duties that evening. It shouldn't take them more than a few hours to get it done, and they'll only need to be available maybe twice a month to do it, but if they're occupied somewhere else, it falls apart. Can you help with this?"

He thought a minute and finally said, "I think I can pull some strings and get that done. The Army isn't going to like it, but technically, I don't work for the Army. They work for me."

I smiled and thanked him.

He then said, "Not to change the subject, but you're scheduled to fly back to Saigon this afternoon, right?"

"Yes sir."

"Well don't miss your flight. Intel tells us that the VC are planning something, and it may be another attack on your ship. Shelling your ship would be quite a feather in their caps. If they start shelling, I'm going to direct the ship to immediately get the hell out of here. That will make your status here a little iffy."

"Thanks for the heads up. I'll definitely be on that flight."

This deal was beginning to seem like trying to play golf when a couple of the obstacles are land mines.

Danessen followed me out. As we walked to the truck, I tried to explain where we were and what he needed to do if I had to leave before this thing was wrapped up. It ended with my giving him the telephone number of where I was working at Chief, Naval Advisory

Group, and I told him to call me with any updates or if he had any problems.

I looked at my watch. It was now 1300. The flight took off in two hours. It was the same flight I came in on.

When we got back to the pier, we parked at the warehouse, and I walked back down the pier to the ship. The sailor on duty said that he had taken a message from a First Sergeant Rollins. He read the message to me.

"He said that there are some things that need to be worked out, but they would like to move forward." Great. I had about an hour before I had to leave for the airport.

I walked back to the warehouse and found Danessen. He stopped what he was doing and looked up when he saw me. I said, "First Sergeant Rollins left a message with the quarterdeck. They are potentially in, but there are some details that need to be worked out. I have to catch that flight back to Saigon today or I may be stuck here a lot longer than I had planned. I need to turn it over to you to meet with them and see if you can work something out. I'll be in Saigon until Sunday, and you can call me there if you need me. You have the basic details."

"I think I can handle it sir."

"I think you can too. It seems like now it's just working through the details. I have the Commander's word that he will try to get you guys sprung from guard duty – at least on the days that you are pulling stuff."

"Thanks for that sir."

"One more thing. I'll need someone to take me to the airport. Can you detail one of your guys?"

"Sure. When do want to leave?"

"About an hour."

"Come back down when you're ready to go."

"See you in about an hour."

The first thing I did was go get my briefcase and shaving kit. If I had to get off the ship quickly, I didn't want to have to waste time getting that stuff. I put them on the quarterdeck. I then went down to the galley. The smell of baking chicken filled the room. Petty Officer Thomas had put colored tablecloths on the tables. Although most of the sailors would vehemently deny it, doing things like putting tablecloths on the tables turned it into a dining room and not a galley. It actually improved the look of the place.

The cook saw me and asked if I was going to have some lunch. I told him I'd try, but I had some things I needed to do and had to leave in about an hour. "Sure smells good though."

In truth, my stomach was churning. I doubted I could keep lunch down even if I tried it. The stress had finally gotten to me. I wasn't at all sure that what I had tried to set in motion was going to work even if it did get set up. If the wrong person got involved and started quoting "the book" this wasn't totally legal, and it was my ass on the line. On the other hand, whoever was in line to complain would have to deny any knowledge of the illegal operation the First Sergeant was running. But then I'd have to answer for why I didn't report it.

I was also worried that I was leaving before it was up and running and had to leave someone to work it out who had little or no experience in this arena. If it blew up because of his inexperience, well, I was still on the hook. There were going to be problems the first couple of times that they went through the process, and a couple of times might be the only times that they ran it. If there were major problems that occurred before the ships pulled out and we shut down, then of course that's all that would be remembered.

And then there was the real possibility that at any minute the VC might start shelling the ship. I actually thought for a moment that if the ship did get shelled and I got hit, I'd get a purple heart, probably a citation. I would be sent back to the States and maybe get out of the Navy on a medical discharge. At that moment, I might have opted for it.

I looked at my watch. I'd been sitting here for about half an hour. I needed to check out. I went to find the CO.

I found him in the wardroom having lunch. He invited me to sit and eat. I declined and used as the excuse that I had to get to the airport. I briefed him on what I'd done and what was still left to be done. He put a bite in his mouth, put his fork down, chewed on it a minute and then asked, "Is this going to work?'

"Well, let me put it this way. It's to everyone's benefit to make it work. All the parts are in place. But it just takes one person to decide that he's not getting the credit for it to fuck it up."

He picked up his fork, put another bite in his mouth chewed it for a minute and said, "Sounds like you've done everything you could do. Let's just hope it works. I'll try to keep an eye on it. I do appreciate your coming over here and trying."

Faint praise, but I took it.

I stopped by the galley and found the Storekeeper there having lunch. I told him that he would be gone before the new procedure could be put in place, but I'd appreciate any assistance he could give. He agreed to help in any way he could. I walked over and shook the cook's hand, wishing him well and headed for the quarterdeck.

I got my stuff, saluted the watch, turned and saluted the flag on the stern and walked down the gangplank. As I walked down the pier toward the warehouse, I was still worried about all of this. Finally, I shrugged thinking that I had tried to do everything I could. It was small consolation.

Next stop – the airport.

I was lost in my own thoughts as we drove back. I didn't even recognize the village that we had driven through only two nights before.

I checked in for the flight and boarded the plane a little while later. The atmosphere on the plane was totally different from the flight down here. The guys on this flight were either going home, going somewhere for a week of R&R, or going to Saigon for a few days – at least temporarily out of harm's way. It was almost a celebration. People talking, joking, laughing.

We landed in Saigon and there was a driver from the Advisory Group to pick me up and take me back to the office. I was sitting at my assigned desk, when I heard someone call my name. I looked up and it was a classmate that I had known in ROTC in college, Gene Thibodeaux. There were only 24 of us in that class. Only 12 of us had become Supply Officers. It was highly unlikely that I would ever run into someone I knew from that time. Thibodeaux had been assigned to Vietnam and was finishing his tour. He was scheduled to return to the States about the same time that I was scheduled to return to Guam. Having been relieved at his duty station, he was temporarily in Saigon completing his out-processing before he returned home. We sat and caught up for a few minutes. He had things he needed to accomplish, so we agreed to meet for dinner later that evening.

He picked me up after work. He knew some of the better restaurants in Saigon, so he selected a French restaurant with a good reputation. He was from South Louisiana, Cajun country, so he was well acquainted with good food. We had a six-course gourmet dinner complete with drinks to start, wine with dinner and brandy to top it off. We caught up, talking about classmates we knew and what had happened to them. I told him about having a couple of our classmates visiting me in the job I had at the shipyard as their ships were passing through Guam on the way back to the States and the unstated questions that they all had, "What had I done to deserve this?" Or more to the point, "Where had they gone wrong." I tried to console them by telling them that what they were doing was far more career enhancing, but since none of them intended to make the Navy a career, it was small, if any, consolation.

Periodically during the meal, it came to mind that just this morning I had been in a combat arena, having experienced everything I had gone through in those few days, not the least of which was making sure I got out before the ship was shelled. Now here I was, sitting in a gourmet restaurant having a truly exceptional meal. Getting my head around all of this was beginning to be challenging. Once again, I just mentally shrugged.

DAY FIVE

I WAS BACK IN SAIGON and back at Chief, Naval Advisory Group Headquarters. The only thing I had left to do was finalize my report. I could have summarized the entire report in two sentences, "The logistics support problem is fucked up and going to stay fucked up so long as our ships have to rely on the Army for support when the Army is pulling out of Vietnam, and the guy that you worked with yesterday may be gone tomorrow. I tried to set up procedures where our support guys would assist in pulling the stuff the ships needed, but I left without it being put into place and I had no idea if it was going to be put into place or would work if it did." However, I needed to draft it in a manner that didn't state the obvious and allowed the person reading the report to draw that conclusion and at the same time it didn't put me on report. Something in the neighborhood of five pages, double spaced, with wide margins and large type should handle the necessary number of pages. The drafting was going to be the hard part.

I was sitting at a desk when Bob, who was scheduled to DEROS (go home) in a week or so, walked in and announced to no one in particular, "I think I've located my dental file. I heard that it was moved to MACV headquarters." He turned to me and asked, "If you're not busy, would you like to go over there with me?" Ascertaining quickly that this was a reprieve from staring at the blank sheet of paper in front of me, I quickly accepted.

As we walked to the Jeep I asked, "What's this about?"

"When you leave here, you have to take out with you everything you brought in. That includes all of your personnel records. With the drawdown, as offices close, records are moved. I've been looking for my Dental Records for several weeks. If you don't have something you are supposed to have, you can be held here until you have it. That also holds true for anything you've signed for. The real problems come up if you're the last in line and leave without a relief and you are required to turn in something that you signed for but have never even seen and don't know if it still exists. There are stories of guys who signed for equipment from someone who signed for the same equipment, and so forth, possibly back for years. None of them ever had the time to check to see if the equipment still existed. With the drawdown, the last guy is getting held until he comes up with the missing item or pays for it. Being short one helicopter, even a small helicopter, can ruin your whole day."

I reminded him that the Navy has backups for medical records. I was again reminded that this was an Army war.

We arrived at MACV headquarters - a large, old French fort with tall, grey, mossy walls surrounding it. We entered through the small gate in the front and were stopped by the ARVN guards at the gate. They checked the Jeep, which included using a rather large mirror attached at a right angle to a pole to look underneath the Jeep for bombs. We entered the compound and parked. The front of the building had a double, curved staircase which went up to the main floor. We went up and found the Navy Admin office. Just like yesterday's warehouse, sailors were crowded around the counter shouting to be heard. Bob approached the counter under the sign indicating "Officer Records" and was seen by a young sailor who pointed at him since he couldn't be heard.

Bob shouted, "I heard that my Dental Records may have been moved over here."

The sailor shouted back, "Go back down the stairs. Turn and go through the walkway between the stairs. It's room 105," was all he said and pointed at the next person.

We went back out and down the stairs, talking as we went. We found Room 105 and continued our conversation expecting the same chaotic situation that existed in the upstairs room. We turned the handle, shoved the door open and barged in. The room was silent. In the room was a single, large wooden desk, and behind the desk set a Naval Dental Captain, a very senior Navy dentist, in a khaki uniform with an eagle on his right collar. He was reading a paperback book. There was nothing else on the desk, nothing else in the office and nothing else going on.

We immediately fell silent.

The captain looked up from his book and quietly asked, "May I help you?"

Obviously, we were in the wrong room. Bob began to stammer and apologize as we quickly backed out of the room while he blamed the sailor upstairs with giving us the wrong room number.

The captain then asked, "What were you looking for?"

Continuing his apology Bob explained that he was looking for his dental records and was directed to this room, but possibly he hadn't heard correctly, or the sailor had the wrong room number or ...

The captain then asked Bob his name.

As Bob was telling him, I noticed a small table beside the desk with a cardboard box on top. After Bob told him his full name, the captain leaned over and thumbed through the contents of the box. He pulled a file out of the box, handed it to Bob and quietly said, "Here it is," and went back to reading his book.

Bob thanked him, and we backed out of the room.

Once outside, we just stood and looked at each other for a moment trying to figure out what had just happened. While shaking my head I asked, "Do you think that's what that son of bitch was sent over here to do?'

Bob responded. "You never can tell. You know it's a pretty fucked-up war."

After lunch I was back at Headquarters and still trying to start my report. I got up to take a piss. The head is down a hall. There are several offices that open onto that hallway. Most have frosted glass windows at the top of the door, with the name of the department along with a logo painted on the glass. I don't recall seeing anyone entering or leaving any of those offices, but since I occasionally ran into sailors I didn't know, mostly while I was in the head, I figured that there must be someone behind those doors. One door particularly interested me. The name said, "Navy Psychological Warfare." My mind immediately went to some kind of interrogation unit, but the security in this building was not the type that I thought would be necessary for the kind of activities that I was imagining. Maybe they were the guys that came up with whatever it was that made me decide to volunteer to come over here in the first place.

When I got back to the office, I asked one of the guys what they did.

"We really don't know for sure. We refer to them as 'pigs and chickens.' All we know is that they give pigs and chickens to the villagers."

About that time, an officer came walking into the room who was introduced to me as being from Psychological Warfare. For some reason, he sat down beside my desk. I surmise that it was because I looked about as busy as I was, that is, not very, and everyone else was occupied. I swiveled my chair to talk to him.

A description of this individual indicated what he might be doing. As I previously said, we were all dressed in Navy khaki uniforms. We didn't carry weapons. By the patch above his pocket I could see that this guy was in the Navy, and by his collar insignia, I saw that he was a lieutenant. He wasn't wearing anything that would indicate that he was assigned to any kind of special forces unit, but what first caught my attention was the uniform he was wearing. It was a camouflage uniform. More to the point, it was what was referred to as "jungle silks." The colors were dark greys and blacks, rather than being the greens and browns of the jungle, and the pattern could best be described as lightning bolts or zig-zags. I had heard that these uniforms were designed for night operations. But of particular interest was that he was wearing a handgun. During this time the Navy still issued .45 semi-automatic pistols. His gun appeared to be a 9 mm. And, he had it quick-draw strapped to his thigh. The idea of this guy going into villages to do PR work seemed pretty unlikely.

During our conversation I found out that he was on his second back-to-back tour in Vietnam. He had been here over 18 months. Making sense of our conversation was difficult. He would stop in the middle of telling me something and jump to another topic. I can best describe it as a gear missing a tooth. As the gear turned, it would slip.

I was about to suggest to him that he might consider taking a tour back in the U.S. You know, taking a job in Hawaii or San Diego for a few years, when from one of the large pockets on the front of his shirt (called a "blouse" over here) a medium-sized, gray squirrel crawled out. It climbed up the front of his blouse and sat on his shoulder. Without missing a beat, he reached in another pocket, pulled out a nut and handed it to the squirrel. The squirrel proceeded to turn the nut in its paws and then started gnawing on it. The lieutenant kept talking the whole time. I am sure that my face reflected the many questions that this was generating. Having one's mouth hanging open is usually a clue.

After a minute or so, he must have realized that I was at best, perplexed. Of all the questions that I had, starting with 'What the fuck?' the one he answered was not part of the list. He paused what he was talking about and all he said by way of explanation was, "Oh him. He lives in there," indicating the pocket.

I never did find out what he did.

That afternoon the Officer-in-Charge, George, asked me if I wanted to go to dinner that night. I willingly agreed.

When I got back to the BOQ the day before, I was still wearing the same uniform that I had on when I went to Vung Tau. I had only taken a change of socks and underwear. Jim said that if I put my uniform on the bed and put a few piastres on top of it, the maids would clean it. When I got back to the BOQ this afternoon, I found the uniform on the bed cleaned, ironed and neatly folded. I wondered if this was some kind of metaphor for the change in me that being back in Saigon had occasioned. I changed into the civilian clothes I had brought and waited for George.

George picked me up and told me that we were going to see if Bob wanted to join us. As we drove, I told George the story of Bob's dental record. We both laughed. I was looking forward to having Bob join us. Dinner with Bob had to be a lot of laughs.

When we got to Bob's room, we knocked on the door and a strange voice inside said, "It's open." We opened the door and went in. The room was dark. Bob was sitting in a corner. He had a look on his face that I can only describe as one of absolute terror. His eyes were open wide and staring straight ahead. He didn't say anything.

George only said, "It got you."

Bob tried to smile and said, "Yeah, I guess it did."

"We're going to dinner. You don't think going with us would help?" He just shook his head, "No".

"You know this will pass." He nodded, "Yes".

"Okay, if you need anything let me know."

All he said was, "Thanks."

We walked out and quietly closed the door behind us.

As we walked down the hall, George started to explain, "This thing normally hits you within a week of your first arriving or about a week before you leave. It's worse at the end. You know you only have a week left and then it's over. The fear of getting killed in your last week here ... well it gets to you. It usually passes, though."

For a moment I wondered why it hadn't gotten to me. Maybe I just didn't have time to think about it. Maybe it was whatever kept me calm on the road to the compound. Whatever it was, I hoped I never had to experience it. I will never forget that look of terror.

DAY SIX

I AWOKE THINKING OF SARAH. The first order of business was to try to quell my erection. I thought of a few of the events of the last few days. That was more than enough for Ebenezer to go to "at ease".

Jim and I showered and dressed. We had breakfast and headed back to the headquarters building. As we drove to the building, I thought of Bob. I wondered what he would be like today.

As we entered the building, the first person I saw was Bob. He was standing with a coffee cup in his hand and instead of khakis was wearing a crisp, white Navy uniform. He was smiling and back to his normal self. He asked about dinner. We talked for a minute as if nothing had occurred the night before. That was as it should be. For now, it never happened, but neither of us would ever forget it.

I got some coffee and sat down at my desk. George came over and asked me about what had happened in Vung Tau. It was good to talk about it to another Supply Officer. I didn't have to do a lot of the explanation I would have to do if I was talking to someone without our training. He sat and listened, nodding occasionally.

When I finished, he said, "You're right that it could still blow up in your face, but it sounds like the best solution under the circumstances."

He paused a minute and then continued, "I have a suggestion. Even though that whole area and your ships are way out of any jurisdiction we might have, we still have influence ... and some rank … and we're here. We are still in the Navy and those are our ships. Call your guys and give them my name and telephone number. Have them call me if they run into a stumbling block. I'll see what I can do. Also, copy us on all your messages so I can keep abreast of what's going on."

No matter how pissed off I could get with the Navy, I still had great admiration and respect for a lot of the people in it. This was one of those projects that most people would run from. The fact that George was willing to get involved meant that his butt was now on the line, too. I couldn't have been more appreciative.

Later that morning I called our warehouse. I got Petty Officer Danessen on the phone.

I started with, "So how's it going?"

"Well I'm in Vietnam trying to do a nearly impossible job with people who don't have any training in what we're supposed to be doing. And, oh yes, there's the possibility of getting my ass blown off. Other than that, everything is great."

I chuckled.

"Have you talked to the Army?"

"Yeah, that first sergeant seems to be fully onboard. I don't know exactly what you said to him, but whatever it was, it worked. My guys start training tomorrow. Hell, this might even work."

"We'll start with the next ship. Can you get up to speed by the time they get there?"

"We'll be as ready as we can be, given that SNAFU is rampant over here."

"I do have a little bit of good news. Get some pencil and paper to write something down."

"I'll be right back."

When he got back on the phone, I told him that the officers that I was working with in Saigon had agreed to monitor this thing and lend assistance when they could. I then gave him the commander's name and telephone number.

"If you run into a snag and need some horsepower call him. Make sure that you copy them on any messages you send out that deal with logistics. Got that?"

"Yes sir. I hope I won't have to call him, but it's great to know I can."

"That's exactly what I thought. Just make sure you use it only when you have done everything you can do. He's putting his ass on the line for us."

"Yes sir."

"I leave tomorrow. I'll check with you when I get back to Guam. Otherwise, have a nice Vietnam day."

He chuckled and we hung up.

I went over to my desk, opened my briefcase and took out a pad of paper. I had written across the top of the first page, "Draft of Report." That was the only thing on the page. I had made some notes on some other sheets, but the sum didn't total much of anything.

My problem was – how was I going to draft a report which effectively set up a procedure that was quasi-legal, if probably not just quasi … without putting myself on report.

One method I had heard of was from a guy who, when faced with a similar problem, quoted regulations that didn't exist as his authority for doing something. The military was rife with weighty manuals which were full of regulations on how almost everything was supposed to be done and, additionally, there were instructions that were handed down, but not really codified any-where. The guy who told me about this was an Army officer I was talking to over dinner who said he would begin by stating that, according to Army Regulation 2507.2(B)3 and then with a flourish stated "and I quote" and then stated whatever it was he wanted it to say.

Since the regulation didn't exist, no one was going to admit that they couldn't find it, even if they went to read it, which they never did. He said he learned the trick in college debate. But in college, he said he'd quote the noted scholar who "clearly stated," and then he'd quote his college roommate. Again, he wasn't challenged because no one wanted to admit that they had never heard of the noted scholar.

I pondered this for a minute and decided that maybe that was a little too much for me. However, I could plead that I hadn't had the time nor the available manuals to verify my memory on the subject, but that I clearly recalled that in exigent circumstances such procedures were lawful. All kinds of things could be done in "exigent circumstances," and just possibly this might be one of them. Surely having to operate in a war that was being "managed" by the Army constituted an exigent circumstance. And what the hell, this entire procedure might be set up to handle the one ship that might be coming in for resupply before all the ships were pulled out of Vietnam. I gave another mental shrug and got down to writing.

I looked up about lunchtime. Since I was heading back to Guam the next day, we all went to lunch together. We talked about going back to the mess where we had eaten lunch the first day.

"Just in case you had such a good time here you were thinking about coming back, we wanted to further entice you with the great food."

Instead we walked to a Vietnamese Restaurant and had Pho.

It struck me how routine this all seemed. I was working on a report which, if it was read at all, would probably be read once, filed and forgotten. During lunch we started talking about possible future duty stations. Some of the officers wanted to know about Guam, so I told them it was a great place to scuba dive, buy things cheap and drink. But it was an island with no available women. Before I arrived in Vietnam, I wasn't at all sure what life in a combat zone would be like, but I never dreamed it would be like this. Duty in Saigon bordered on dull.

I spent the afternoon talking to the other officers and working on my report. I wondered how many times I could include the words, "exigent circumstances" in it before it would call attention to itself.

That night Jim and I went back to the bar that we had gone to the night I got here. It now seemed an eon ago, but it was in reality less than a week. The pregnant girl wasn't there. I wondered if she had had her baby.

As I stood at the bar drinking my beer, another of the girls walked up and said, "Hello Dai Uy. You very handsome man."

"Dai Uy" was the Vietnamese term for a lieutenant. I wasn't in uniform so how she knew that I was a lieutenant was anyone's guess. I later found out that if you looked like you might be an officer, to them you were now a Dai Uy. I thanked her.

She continued, "Handsome man like you need girlfriend. You think me pretty. I could be girlfriend." I told her I appreciated her offer, but I was leaving tomorrow.

"What time you leave tomorrow?"

"I leave for the airport about 0500."

"Okay I be your girlfriend forever … or maybe only until 0500 tomorrow."

The laugh was worth the few piastres I gave her.

Back at the BOQ, I lay awake in my bunk mentally sorting through the last several days. None of it made any sense. As images came to mind, I started chuckling, which morphed into full-fledged laughter. In a short while I was laughing so hard that tears came streaming down my cheeks. My roommate rolled over and asked, "What the fuck are you laughing at?"

"I don't really know for sure. Me, I guess. Vietnam, I guess. Probably all of it." I didn't say anymore, but I knew that whatever the actual reason was, I had just realized how insane it all had been and that no one could have made up all this stuff.

I turned over and tried to stifle, but an occasional chuckle still wormed its way out.

DAY SEVEN

I was scheduled to return to Guam today. I couldn't believe that I had only been here for a week, but also it didn't seem like I had been here only a week. I was still trying to get my head around everything that had gone on. I still didn't understand it. Maybe what I had tried to do would make some difference … but who knows.

I got on the plane, stored my bag in the overhead locker and kept my briefcase. I intended to try to do some more work on the report. I moved into the window seat.

The atmosphere on the plane was 180 degrees out from the atmosphere on the plane that brought me to Saigon that first day. Most of these soldiers were either going home or going on R&R. They were talking, joking and laughing. They were flirting with the stewardesses. I didn't imagine that many of them would be sober when they landed – wherever they were going.

"Excuse me, sir."

I looked up. A young Army soldier was standing in the aisle. He was probably in his early 20s, maybe younger.

"I want to sit in the window seat."

A sergeant standing in the aisle told him to just sit in the first available seat. I cut him off.

"It's okay. I'm getting off at Guam. I've seen plenty of ocean, and looking out the window at this one doesn't particularly interest me. If he wants to watch the ocean, it's fine with me."

The soldier didn't say anything else to me as I moved into the aisle to let him in.

It was then that I looked at him. I mean really looked at him. His face didn't reflect a sense of relief. He didn't seem pleased to be getting on this plane. His face was almost expressionless. I can only describe it as the way I would imagine someone looked when they had been through an ordeal and, although they survived it, it still haunted them. He didn't thank me, he just moved to the seat, sat down, turned and looked out the window.

When it came time to take off, the stewardess came by and told him to buckle his seat belt. He sat there as if he hadn't heard her. I tapped his shoulder and, nodding at his seat belt, I told him he needed to buckle it. It took him a minute to understand what I had just told him. Again, without saying anything, he buckled his seat belt and went back to looking out the window. He stayed that way for the whole flight to Guam. At one point, I offered to buy him a drink. He didn't respond. Wherever he was, I'm not sure he even heard me. He just sat and stared out the window.

As I sat there trying to work, my mind kept returning to this soldier sitting next to me. What had he seen? What was it that he had he experienced? Even though most of us never actually experienced combat, there were other demons that could capture your soul in Southeast Asia – drugs, alcohol, even the loneliness. Close friends you made today were gone in a week.

I wondered what he was like before he came to Vietnam. For some reason my mind started formulating a background for this guy. He was not yet 20 years old. His ribbon bar didn't show anything that would indicate that he had been in combat. He was probably from a small town and joined the military right out of high school. He had seen lots of war movies. America always won. He was ready to go and fight and die for his country. He wasn't prepared for what it was really like. Some of the good guys died. Some in combat, some from overdoses – either accidental or intentional. When he told his girlfriend that he had signed up, she had thought it was stupid and had probably already moved on.

That wasn't the way it was supposed be. Nothing made any sense.

I began to wonder what his life was going to be like. Would he ever get past whatever this was that was haunting him? If it was drugs or booze, he was taking the demon back with him. How many other soldiers like him were we sending home this way? Would anyone back in the States understand what it was really like? Probably not.

I recalled my college roommate. His college deferment from the draft was about to expire. He was terrified of getting drafted and being sent to Vietnam. At a party one night, one of the women was holding forth on her inability to "find herself." She had decided that she was going to drop out of school and take a year off and go travel in Europe. No, they wouldn't understand.

I thought about this week. It didn't make much sense, but I was going back to Guam, and there was someone there who would be glad to see me. I knew I was different from the experience, but I was okay.

When I got to Guam, she was there waiting for me.

Regardless of how long you had been there, it changed each of us. For a few of us, war was hell. For the rest of us, Vietnam was insanity.

EPILOGUE

By the end of that summer, Barbie had gone home and filed for divorce; the ships had been pulled out of Vietnam; and the procedure I had set up had worked – exactly twice.

For the remainder of the time I had on Guam, Sarah and I continued to see each other as often as we could. We discussed our future together and concluded, that with her baby, we really didn't have one.

The following fall I turned 25.

I left the island in June of the next year. I had asked Sarah not to come to the airport to see me off. For all that time, we had been able to keep our affair from being found out. I was worried that if she came to the airport neither of us would be able to keep it together and with my friends who would be there – well, the risks of blowing it at the end were just too great.

I boarded the plane and sat next to the window. I stowed my suitcase, buckled my seat belt and then turned and looked out the window. Sarah and her baby were standing in the parking lot up against the fence. The plane was too far away for her to see me, but as I choked up, I mouthed, "Thank you."

I never saw her again.

The plane flew to Travis Air Force Base outside of San Francisco. As a result of the news we got on Guam, I fully expected to be met with protestors who would take great pleasure in vilifying me. There weren't any.

On the day I was processed off active duty I went to visit a high school classmate who was then living in the Bay Area. He had managed to keep from getting drafted by receiving a medical deferment, which he probably faked. Even though it was 10:00 in the morning, he broke open a bottle of champagne. We celebrated my returning and his not going. I have never held any ill will against the people who managed to stay out of that war. Dying for someone else's mistake only compounds the mistake.

For many years I listened to Vietnam vets tell how we could have won the war – that the politicians kept us from winning. I usually just listened and avoided asking the question that I was always thinking but was never answered. "How would you know if we won?"

Almost four decades later I was sitting in a park next to a retired Naval officer. We both brought our dogs to the park and had gotten to be friends. One day as we were discussing what we had done in the Navy, it suddenly became clear that he was the Commander in charge of the Swift Boats that I had reported to in Vung Tau. He did two tours in Vietnam. I surmised that he was probably one of those individuals who thought we could have won that war. Not wanting to change my opinion of a man I had grown to like and respect, I never asked.

One day as we were sitting there, a young woman came up and asked how we had met. I grinned and said, "Well we probably met in Vietnam in 1972." She then hesitated a moment and then said, "Uh … what did you think about that war?" Literally in unison we answered, "It was a mistake."

Yes, they'll never understand, but maybe I don't either.

GLOSSARY

AK-47   AK-47 is the military designation for an
                assault rifle first designed and put into use in
                the Soviet Union. The weapon is also known
                as a Khalashikov, after its designer, Mikhail
                Khalashnikov. The weapon fires in automatic
                mode. It is the most widely used assault weapon
                in the world.

ARVN   The Army of the Republic of Vietnam. The
                South Vietnamese military.

BOQ   Bachelor Officers Quarters. Although the name
                indicates that these are quarters for unmarried
                officers, they are actually quarters used by any
                officer who was traveling unaccompanied,
                regardless of his or her marital status. As
                a result BOQs are now often referred to as
                Unaccompanied Housing.

Brow   The Navy term for the gangplank.

Captain   In the Navy the term Captain is both a rank and
                a position. The rank of Captain is the equivalent
                of a colonel in the Army, Air Force and Marines.
                An officer who commands a commissioned ship
                in the Navy is also called a captain, regardless of
                his rank. He is also often referred to as the CO,
                short for Commaning Officer and occasionally
                called, the "Skipper".

Command	A command is an Naval military organization. The commanding officer is the person in charge of a command.
Commander	In the Navy the term Commander is both a rank and a position. The rank of Commander is the equivalent of a Lieutenant Colonel in the Army, Air Force and Marines. The term commander is often used to denote the officer in charge of a command not involving a ship.
CSO	Chief Staff Officer. The second in command of a Naval operation which is not a ship.
DEROS	(Pronounced Dee Rohs) Acronym for "Date Estimated Return from Overseas". In Vietnam a DEROS date was the date that a soldier or sailor's obligated time in Vietnam was completed and he or she was scheduled to return to the States. It was also used to mean the act of being separated and being returned to the States. As in, "When do you DEROS?"
Executive Officer	The second in command of a Navy ship.
Fantail	The wide stern area of a ship.
Ho Chi Minh Trail	The route that was used by the North Vietnamese to ferry supplies into South Vietnam.
Huey	A military helicopter. Specifically, the Bell UH-1 Iroquois, nicknamed the "Huey" by the military.

Indochina	Indochina (also known as French Indochina) was originally a region made up of the countries of Vietnam, Laos and Cambodia and were under French rule until 1950 when the three countries became independent of France. The term Indochina came from the Indochina penisula of Southeast Asia which encompasses Myanmar (Burma), Cambodia, Laos, part of Malasia, Thailand and Vietnam.
M-16	M-16 is the military designation for an assault rifle, first used by the U.S. Military in Vietnam. The M-16 can be fired in a semi-automatic mode (the trigger must be pulled each time a bullet is fired) or in fully automatic mode (like a "machine gun"). Gun manufacturers now sell a civilian model of the M-16 named the AR-15, which only fires in a semi-automatic mode and is loved by those individuals who imagine themselves playing soldier.
MACV	Military Assistance Command Vietnam. The Military Assistance Command was the joint service command in charge of all U.S. Military Operations in Vietnam. The Commander was always an Army General.
MPC	A Military Payment Certificate. A form of U.S. currency issued in Vietnam to military personnel. MPCs could only be used in official government activities. They were issued to prevent the the devaluation of Vietnamese currency by keeping U.S. dollars out of general circulation.
Petty Officer	A Navy term for a non-commissioned officer. A Petty Officer is equivalent in rank to a sergeant, which is a better known rank.

PG	A Patrol Gunboat. The PGs used in Vietnam were originally designed for Caribbean patrols but were found to be successful when used in the coastal areas of Vietnam. The hull was made of aluminum and the structure above the hull (the superstructure) was mostly made of fiberglass. The main propulsion system were two diesel engines, but the ships also carrried a jet engine aboard to provide hot gases to turn a turbine which was geared to the ship's propellor to be used for high speed operations. The propellor allowed the ship to go from full speed to a dead stop in less than two lengths of the ship. the ships were manned by 24 men, four officers and 20 enlisted sailors.
Pho	A Vietnamese soup.
Piastre	The Vietnamese currency at the time of this book.
R&R	Rest and relaxation. A vacation or short respite.
Saigon	At the time of this story, Saigon was the capital of South Vietnam. Once the war was over the name was changed to Ho Chi Minh City.
Side Arm	A pistol. Normally a .45 caliber, semi-automatic pistol
SNAFU	Acronym for "Situation Nomal, All Fucked Up".
VC	The Viet Cong. Also referred to as "Charlie" from the military phonetic alphabet where the letters VC were read as Victor Charlie.
Zumi	The nickname give Admiral Zumwalt, who was the senior admiral in the Navy at the time. His title was Chief of Naval Operations.

ABOUT THE AUTHOR

William Michael Murray, who goes by his middle name, is a writer living in Austin, Texas. He draws on his colorful experiences in the military and during four decades of the practice of law to create the vibrant characters, places and stories in his works of fiction.

Michael was born and raised in San Antonio, where he attended public school. His father was in the Navy and was stationed aboard the Battleship Texas on D-Day. After graduating from Alamo Heights High School, Michael earned a bachelor's degree in English from Tulane University and a law degree from St. Mary's University. He has also completed graduate work in the College of Business at the University of Texas in San Antonio.

Upon graduation from Tulane University in 1969, Michael was commissioned as an Ensign in the Navy Supply Corps and received orders to the Supply Corps School in Athens, Georgia. Upon his successful completion of the basic Supply Officer training course, he received orders to the Navy Ship Repair Facility on Guam. He agreed to extend his stay on Guam for an additional year in order to continue to serve at the Ship Repair Facility, but was ordered to the staff of Coastal Squadron Three headquartered in Guam as the Staff Supply Officer. It was during this tour of duty that he volunteered for a mission to Vietnam. The experiences he had during that week formed the basis of his first book, "A Week in Vietnam".

Michael left active duty in June of 1973 and attended law school at St. Mary's University in San Antonio. He graduated in the summer of 1975 and received his license to practice law in Texas.

While in law school, Michael was contacted by the Navy Reserve and was recruited to become a member of the active Naval Reserve. He accepted and, over the next 22 years, had many interesting and varied assignments. He developed a specialty in Navy fuel operations that resulted in several tours in the Pentagon. He retired as a Captain from the Naval Reserve in 1996. He retired from the active practice of law in 2017 to pursue a lifelong dream of writing.

Michael now lives in Austin with his wife, Helen, and their two dogs, Maggie and Dewey. They continue to collect new adventures while traveling in their RV.

A Week in Vietnam is Michael's first published novel.

If you enjoyed this book and would like to keep in touch with Michael, please visit his website, (www.williammichaelmurray.com) and leave your name and email address. He will notify you when his next book is due to be released and will also let you know if he is scheduled to do any book signings or readings in your area. Michael will periodically post original short stories to the site that you can download for free. The website also has an area where you can leave a review of the book and other comments. Michael would sincerely like to know what you thought of the book. You can also stay in touch through his Facebook page, **William Michael Murray Author**.

www.ingramcontent.com/pod-product-compliance
Lightning Source LLC
Chambersburg PA
CBHW020631130626
46552CB00003B/1167